SMURF SO

Peyo

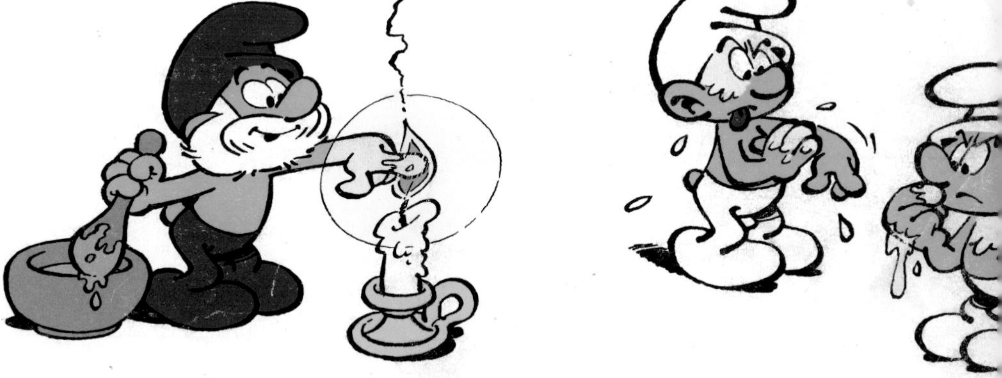

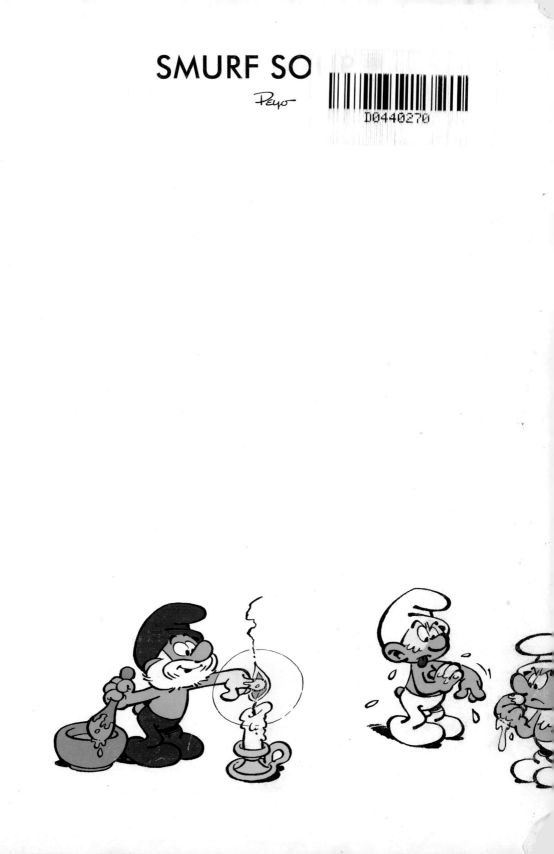

MURF SOUP

Yes, but hey! My soup?
I'm on it!
With ardor, let's smurf together
This ode to our big visitor
He who has smurfed to our
Smurf can be read on his vis
He smurfs with a determined
Ah! There's the big vat!
Okay! Set it down there!
Say, Papa Smurf, you're not really going to make Smurf soup?
Of course! Why not?
10

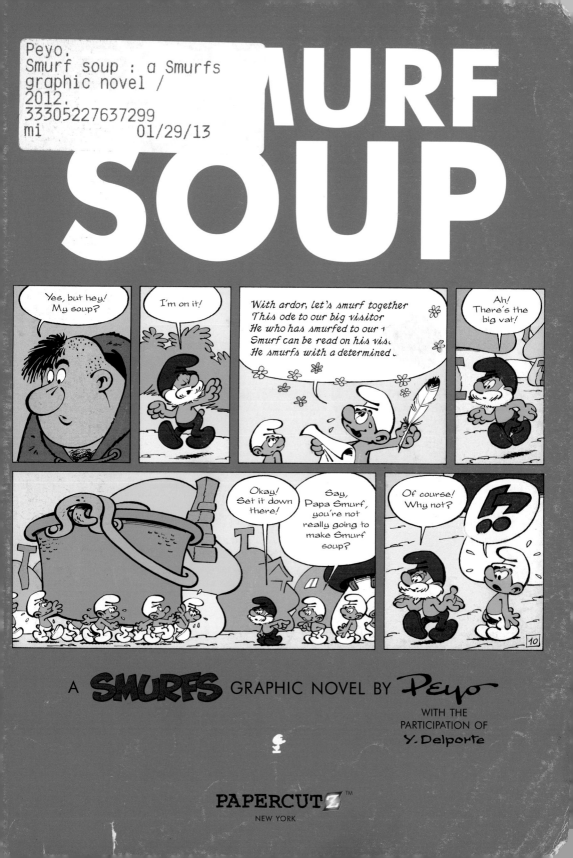

A SMURFS GRAPHIC NOVEL BY PEYO

WITH THE PARTICIPATION OF Y. DELPORTE

PAPERCUTZ™
NEW YORK

SMURFS GRAPHIC NOVELS AVAILABLE FROM PAPERCUTZ™

COMING SOON:

THE SMURFS graphic novels are available in paperback for $5.99 each and in hardcover for $10.99 each at booksellers everywhere. Or order from us. Please add $4.00 for postage and handling for the first book, add $1.00 for each additional book. Please make check payable to NBM Publishing. Send to: PAPERCUTZ, 160 Broadway, Suite 700, East Wing, New York, NY 10038 (1-800-886-1223)

THE SMURFS graphic novels are also available digitally from **COMIXOLOGY**.com.

WWW.PAPERCUTZ.COM

SMURF SOUP

© Peyo - 2012 - Licensed through Lafig Belgium - www.smurf.com

English translation copyright © 2012 by Papercutz.
All rights reserved.

"Smurf Soup"
BY PEYO WITH THE PARTICIPATION
OF YVAN DELPORTE

"Gargamel and the Crocodile"
BY PEYO

"The Clockwork Smurf"
BY PEYO

Joe Johnson, SMURFLATIONS
Adam Grano, SMURFIC DESIGN
Janice Chiang, LETTERING SMURFETTE
Matt. Murray, SMURF CONSULTANT
Michael Petranek, ASSOCIATE SMURF
Jim Salicrup, SMURF-IN-CHIEF

PAPERBACK EDITION ISBN: 978-1-59707-358-5
HARDCOVER EDITION ISBN: 978-1-59707-359-2

PRINTED IN CHINA NOVEMBER 2012 BY WKT CO. LTD.
3/F PHASE I LEADER INDUSTRIAL CENTRE
188 TEXACO ROAD, TSEUN WAN, N.T., HONG KONG

DISTRIBUTED BY MACMILLAN
FIRST PAPERCUTZ PRINTING

SMURF SOUP

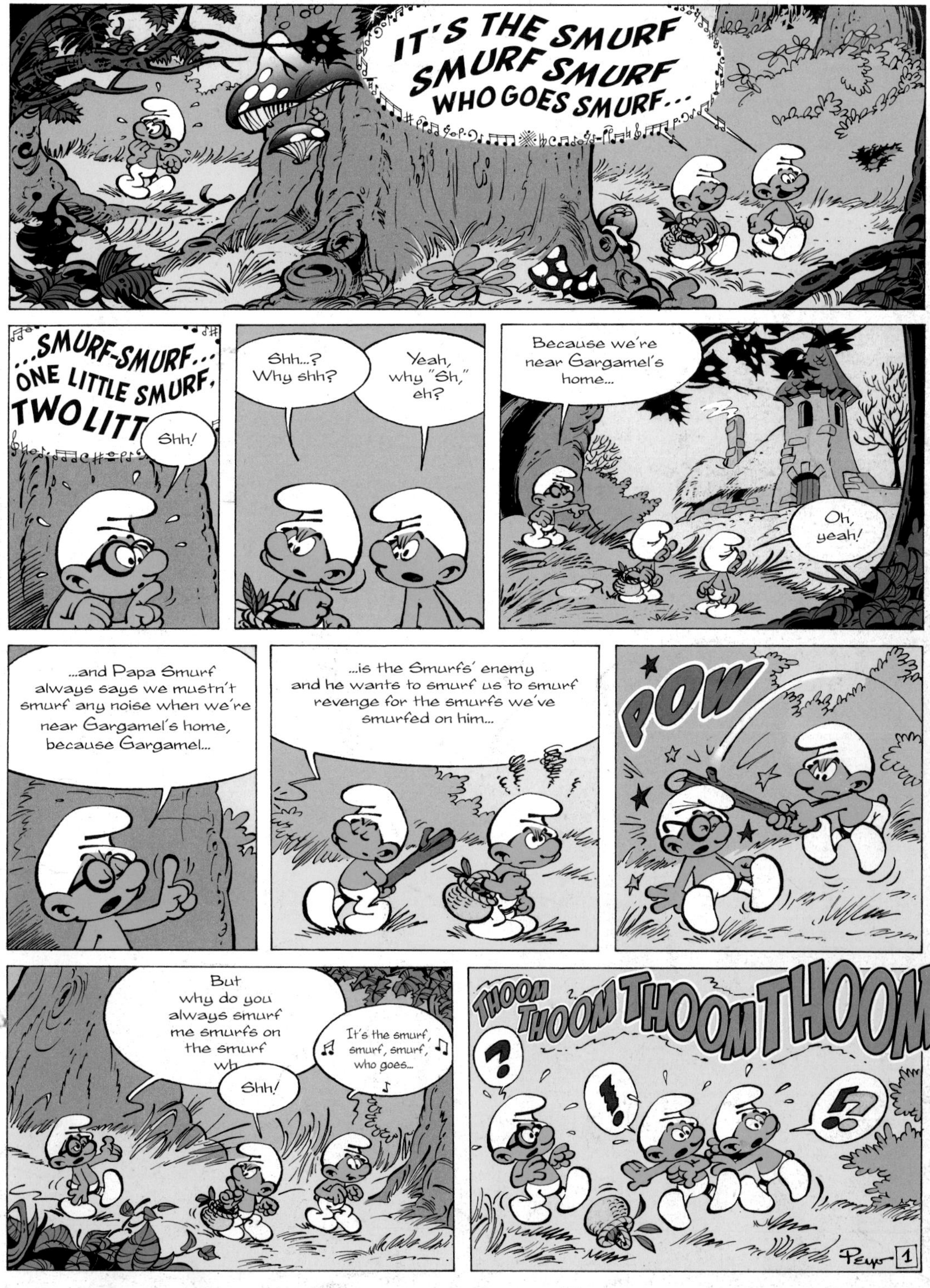
IT'S THE SMURF SMURF SMURF WHO GOES SMURF...
...SMURF-SMURF... ONE LITTLE SMURF, TWO LITT
Shh!
Shh...? Why shh?
Yeah, why "Sh," eh?
Because we're near Gargamel's home...
Oh, yeah!
...and Papa Smurf always says we mustn't smurf any noise when we're near Gargamel's home, because Gargamel...
...is the Smurfs' enemy and he wants to smurf us to smurf revenge for the smurfs we've smurfed on him...
POW
But why do you always smurf me smurfs on the smurf wh
Shh!
It's the smurf, smurf, smurf, who goes...
THOOM THOOM THOOM THOOM
?
!
!?
Peyo
1

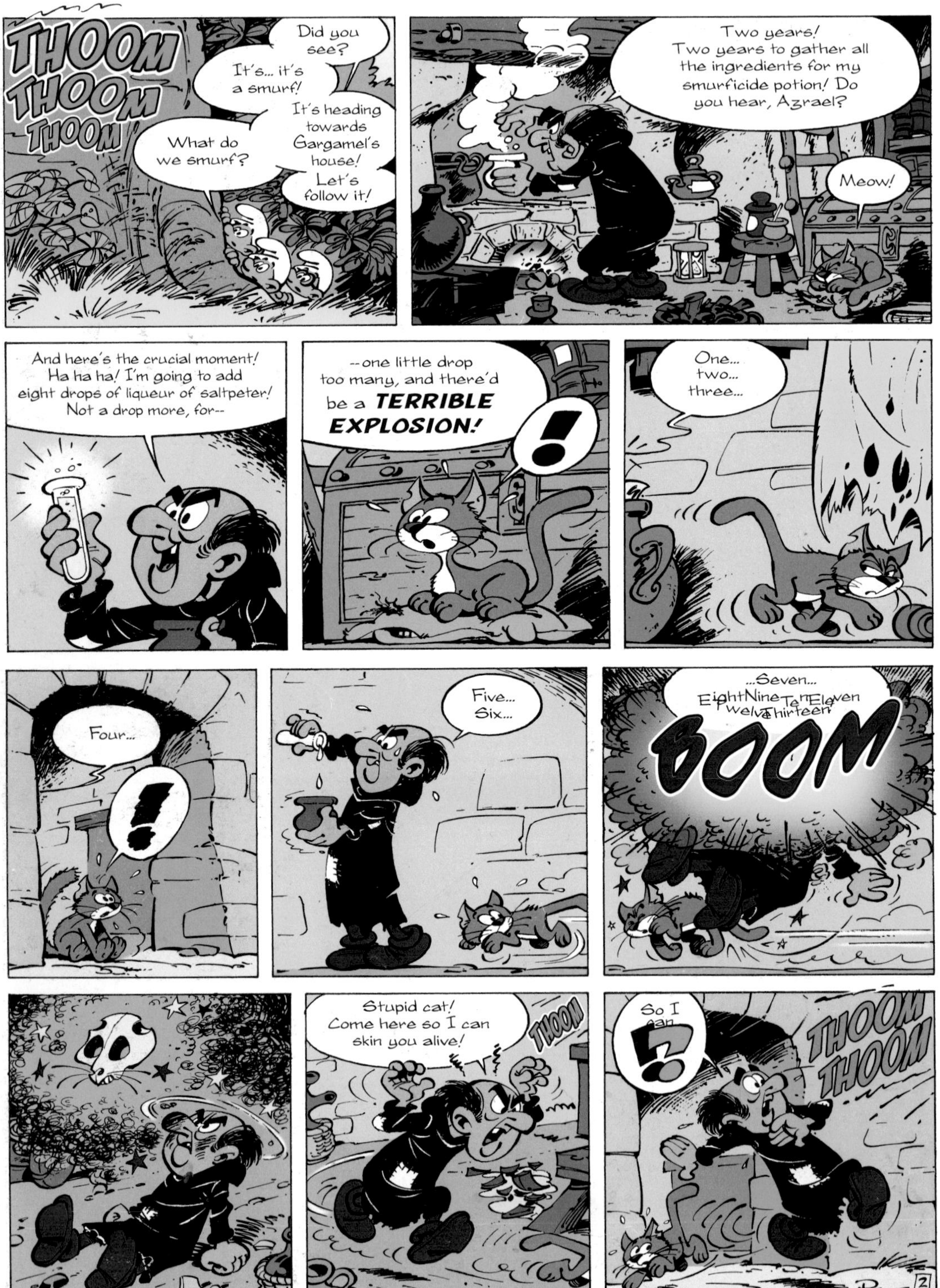
THOOM THOOM THOOM
Did you see?
It's... it's a smurf!
It's heading towards Gargamel's house!
What do we smurf?
Let's follow it!
Two years! Two years to gather all the ingredients for my smurficide potion! Do you hear, Azrael?
Meow!
And here's the crucial moment! Ha ha ha! I'm going to add eight drops of liqueur of saltpeter! Not a drop more, for--
--one little drop too many, and there'd be a TERRIBLE EXPLOSION!
!
One... two... three...
Four...
!
Five... Six...
...Seven...
Eight Nine Ten Eleven Twelve Thirteen
BOOM
Stupid cat! Come here so I can skin you alive!
THOOM
So I
?
THOOM THOOM
Peyo
2

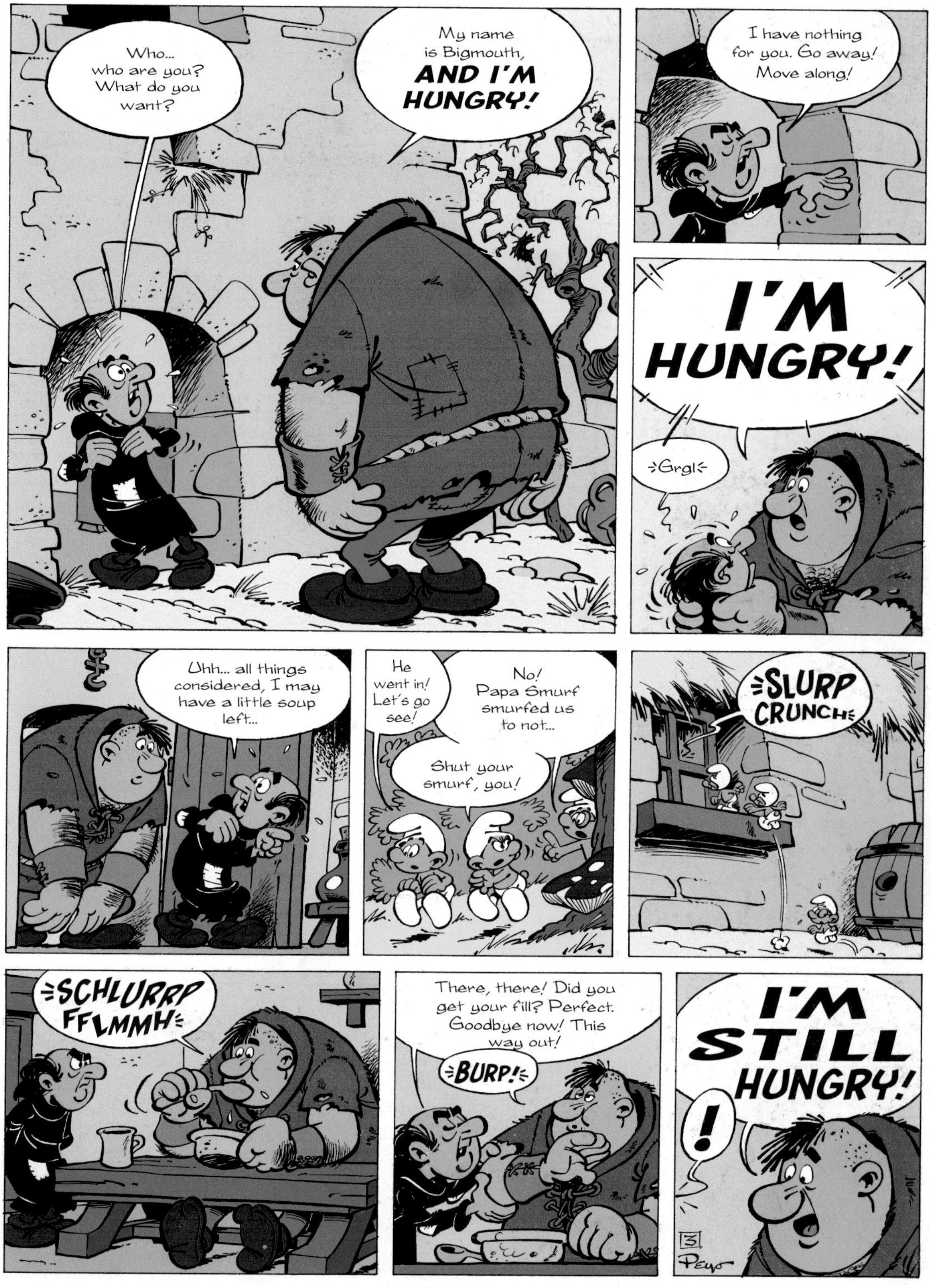

Who... who are you? What do you want?
My name is Bigmouth, AND I'M HUNGRY!
I have nothing for you. Go away! Move along!
I'M HUNGRY!
Grgl
Uhh... all things considered, I may have a little soup left...
He went in! Let's go see!
No! Papa Smurf smurfed us to not...
Shut your smurf, you!
SLURP CRUNCH
SCHLURRP FFLMMH
There, there! Did you get your fill? Perfect. Goodbye now! This way out!
BURP!
I'M STILL HUNGRY!
!

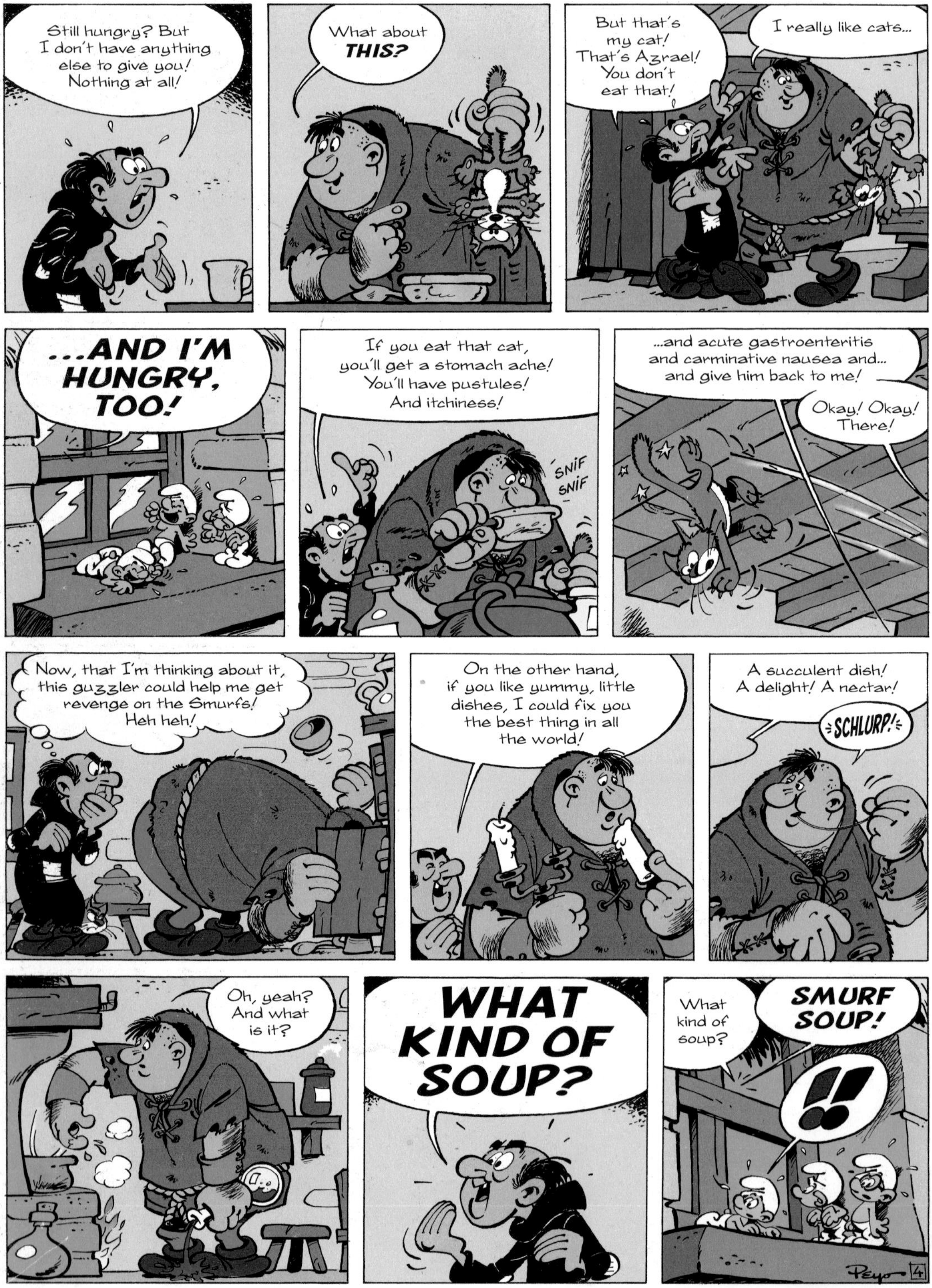
Still hungry? But I don't have anything else to give you! Nothing at all!
What about THIS?
But that's my cat! That's Azrael! You don't eat that!
I really like cats...
...AND I'M HUNGRY, TOO!
If you eat that cat, you'll get a stomach ache! You'll have pustules! And itchiness!
SNIF SNIF
...and acute gastroenteritis and carminative nausea and... and give him back to me!
Okay! Okay! There!
Now, that I'm thinking about it, this guzzler could help me get revenge on the Smurfs! Heh heh!
On the other hand, if you like yummy, little dishes, I could fix you the best thing in all the world!
A succulent dish! A delight! A nectar!
SCHLURP!
Oh, yeah? And what is it?
WHAT KIND OF SOUP?
What kind of soup?
SMURF SOUP!
!!
Peyo
4

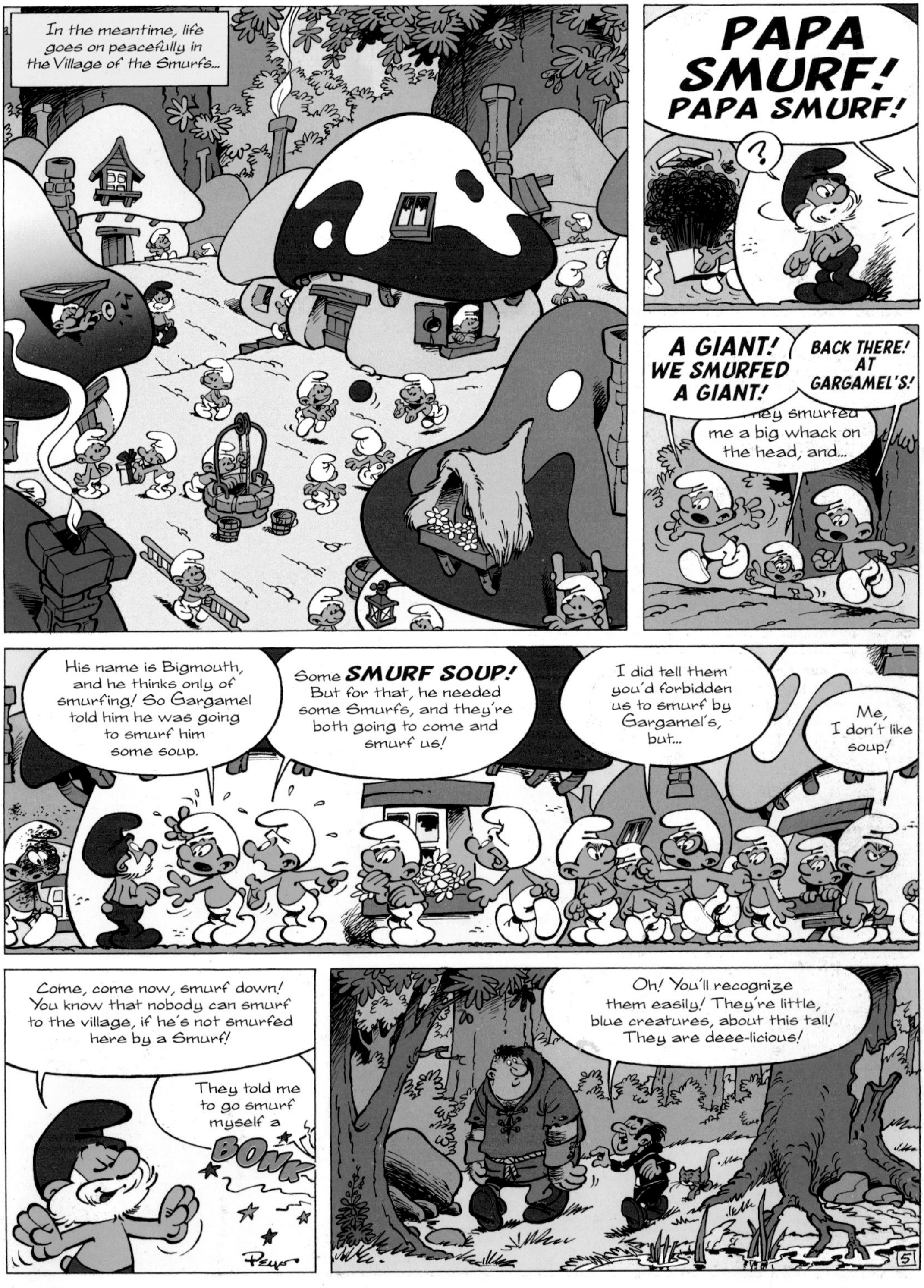
In the meantime, life goes on peacefully in the Village of the Smurfs...
PAPA SMURF! PAPA SMURF!
?
A GIANT! WE SMURFED A GIANT!
BACK THERE! AT GARGAMEL'S!
...hey smurfed me a big whack on the head, and...
His name is Bigmouth, and he thinks only of smurfing! So Gargamel told him he was going to smurf him some soup.
Some SMURF SOUP! But for that, he needed some Smurfs, and they're both going to come and smurf us!
I did tell them you'd forbidden us to smurf by Gargamel's, but...
Me, I don't like soup!
Come, come now, smurf down! You know that nobody can smurf to the village, if he's not smurfed here by a Smurf!
They told me to go smurf myself a
BONK
Oh! You'll recognize them easily! They're little, blue creatures, about this tall! They are deee-licious!
5

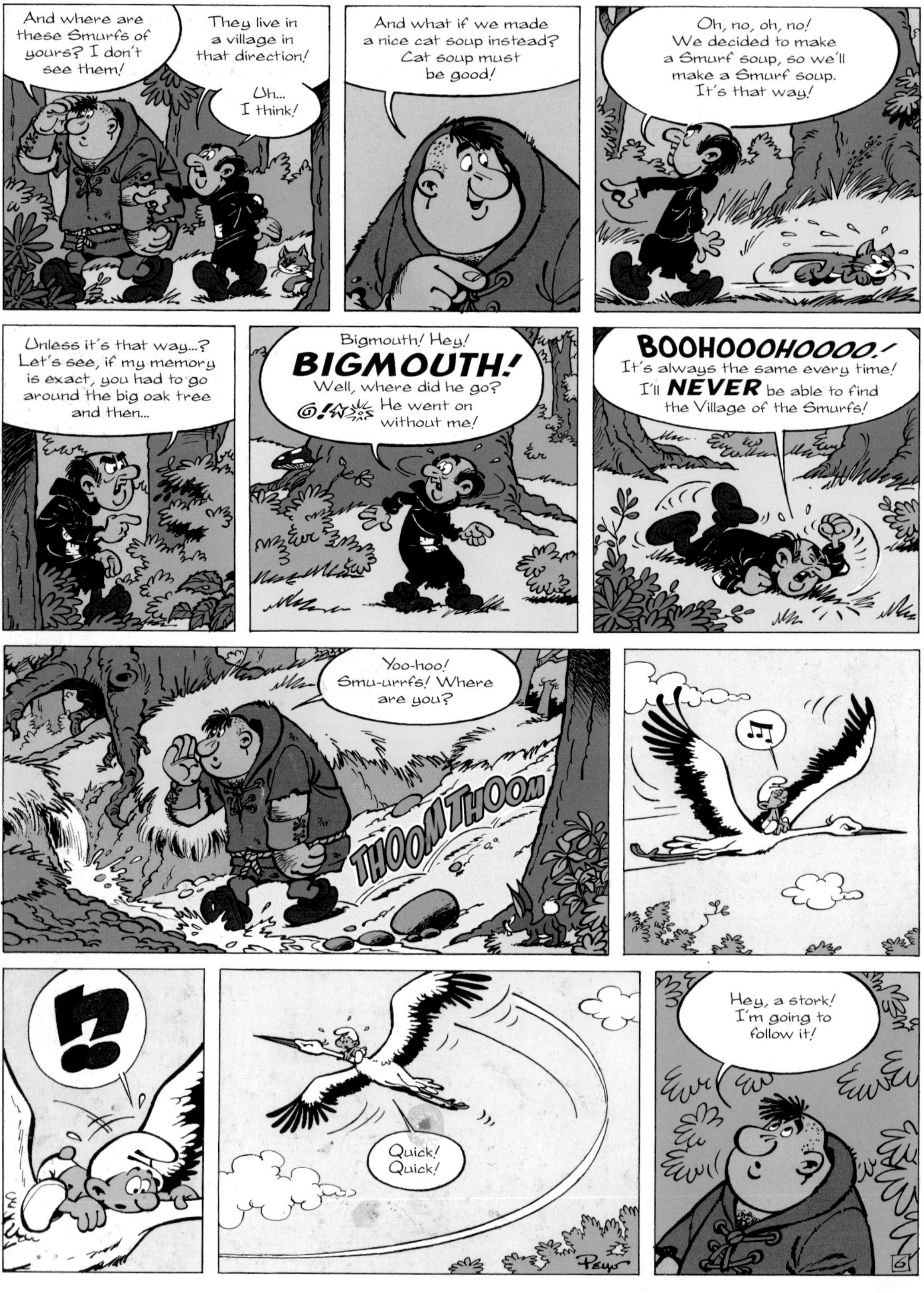
And where are these Smurfs of yours? I don't see them!
They live in a village in that direction!
Uh... I think!
And what if we made a nice cat soup instead? Cat soup must be good!
Oh, no, oh, no! We decided to make a Smurf soup, so we'll make a Smurf soup. It's that way!
Unless it's that way...? Let's see, if my memory is exact, you had to go around the big oak tree and then...
Bigmouth! Hey! BIGMOUTH! Well, where did he go?
He went on without me!
BOOHOOOHOOOO! It's always the same every time! I'll NEVER be able to find the Village of the Smurfs!
Yoo-hoo! Smu-urrfs! Where are you?
THOOM THOOM
Quick! Quick!
Hey, a stork! I'm going to follow it!

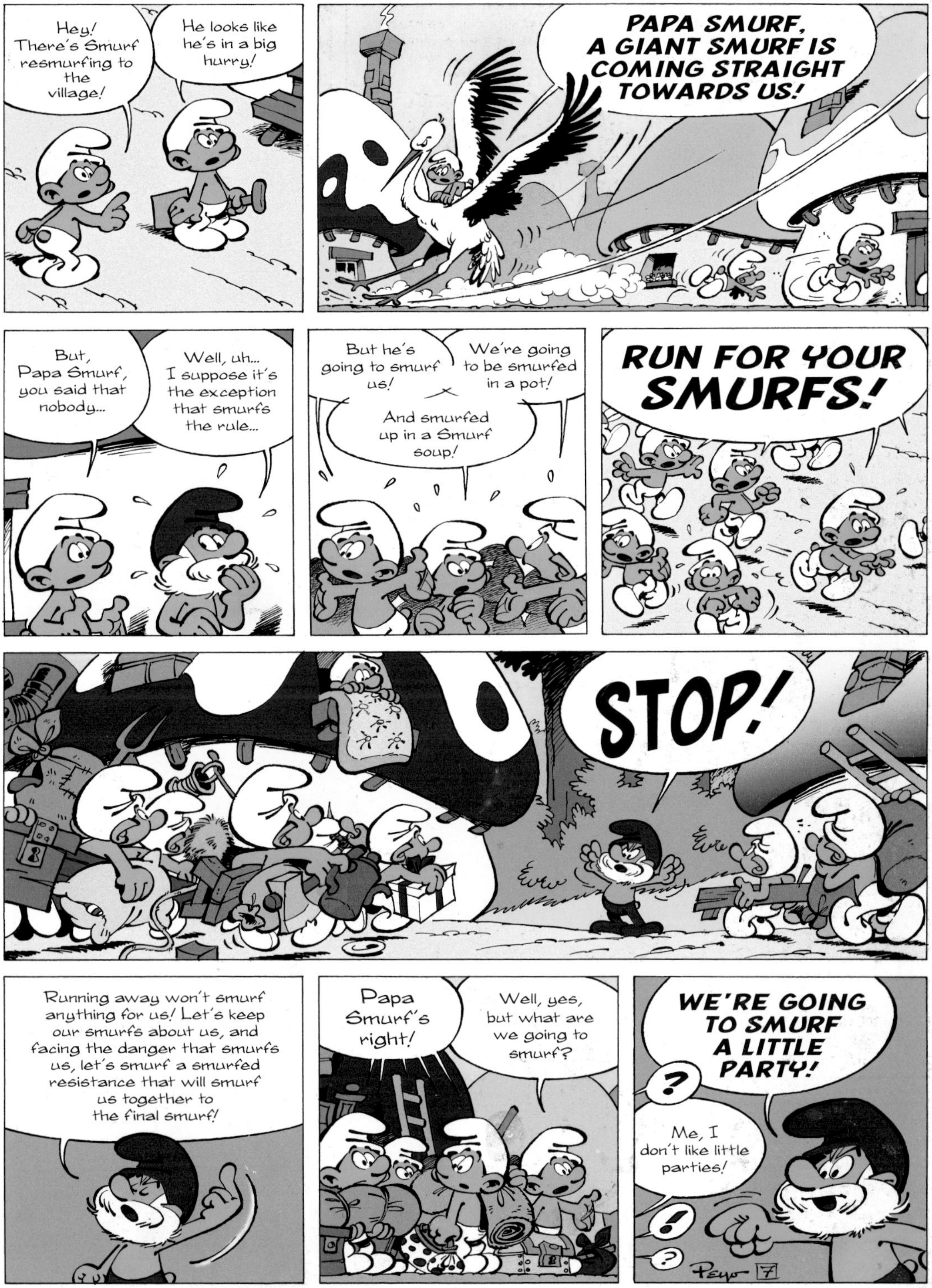

Hey! There's Smurf resmurfing to the village!
He looks like he's in a big hurry!
PAPA SMURF, A GIANT SMURF IS COMING STRAIGHT TOWARDS US!
But, Papa Smurf, you said that nobody...
Well, uh... I suppose it's the exception that smurfs the rule...
But he's going to smurf us!
We're going to be smurfed in a pot!
And smurfed up in a Smurf soup!
RUN FOR YOUR SMURFS!
STOP!
Running away won't smurf anything for us! Let's keep our smurfs about us, and facing the danger that smurfs us, let's smurf a smurfed resistance that will smurf us together to the final smurf!
Papa Smurf's right!
Well, yes, but what are we going to smurf?
WE'RE GOING TO SMURF A LITTLE PARTY!
?
Me, I don't like little parties!
!
?
Peyo 7

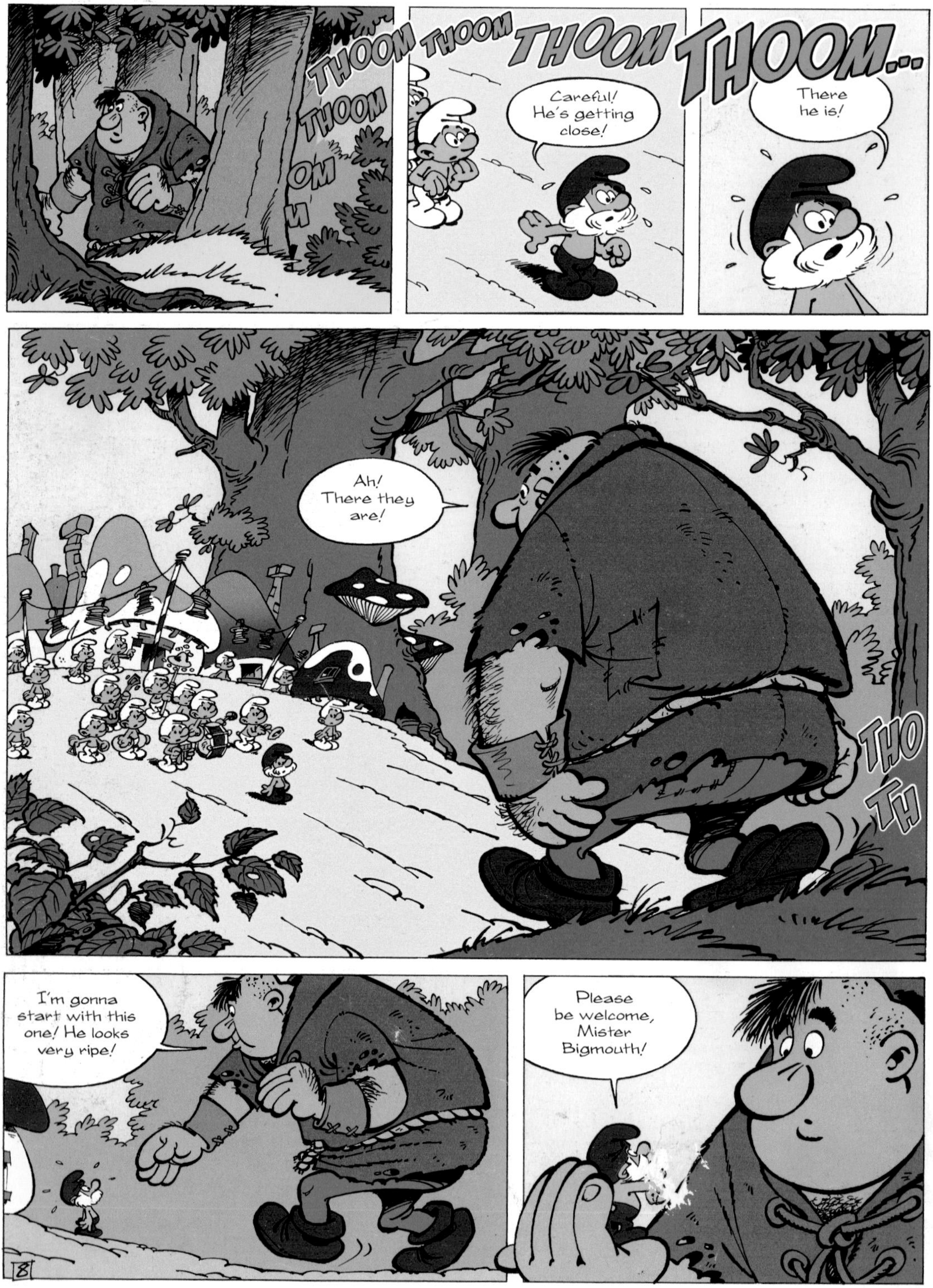
THOOM THOOM
THOOM
OM
THOOM
Careful! He's getting close!
THOOM...
There he is!
Ah! There they are!
THO
TH
I'm gonna start with this one! He looks very ripe!
8
Please be welcome, Mister Bigmouth!

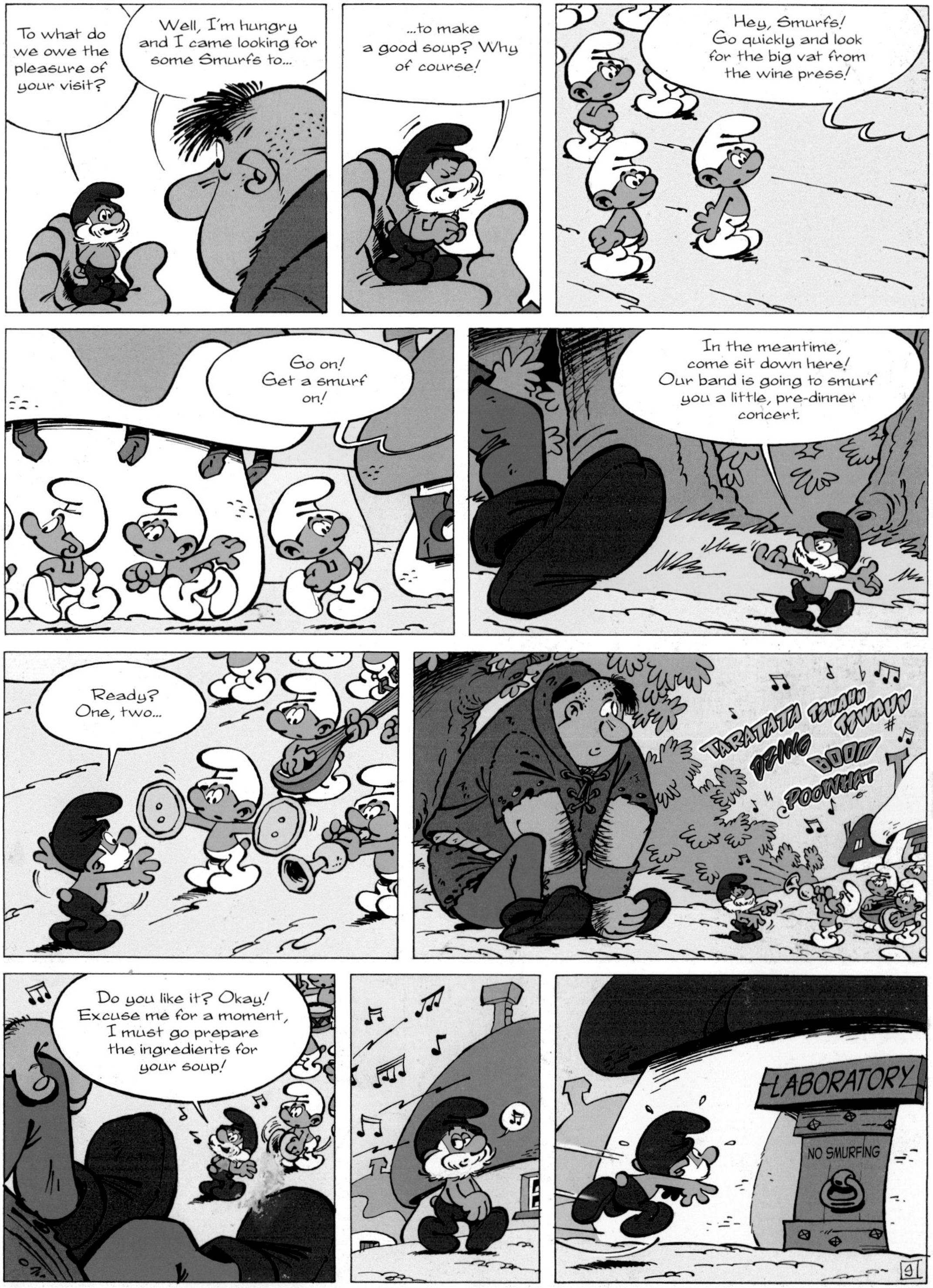
To what do we owe the pleasure of your visit?
Well, I'm hungry and I came looking for some Smurfs to...
...to make a good soup? Why of course!
Hey, Smurfs! Go quickly and look for the big vat from the wine press!
Go on! Get a smurf on!
In the meantime, come sit down here! Our band is going to smurf you a little, pre-dinner concert.
Ready? One, two...
TARATATA TZWAHN TZWAHN DZING BOOM POOWHAT
Do you like it? Okay! Excuse me for a moment, I must go prepare the ingredients for your soup!
LABORATORY
NO SMURFING
9

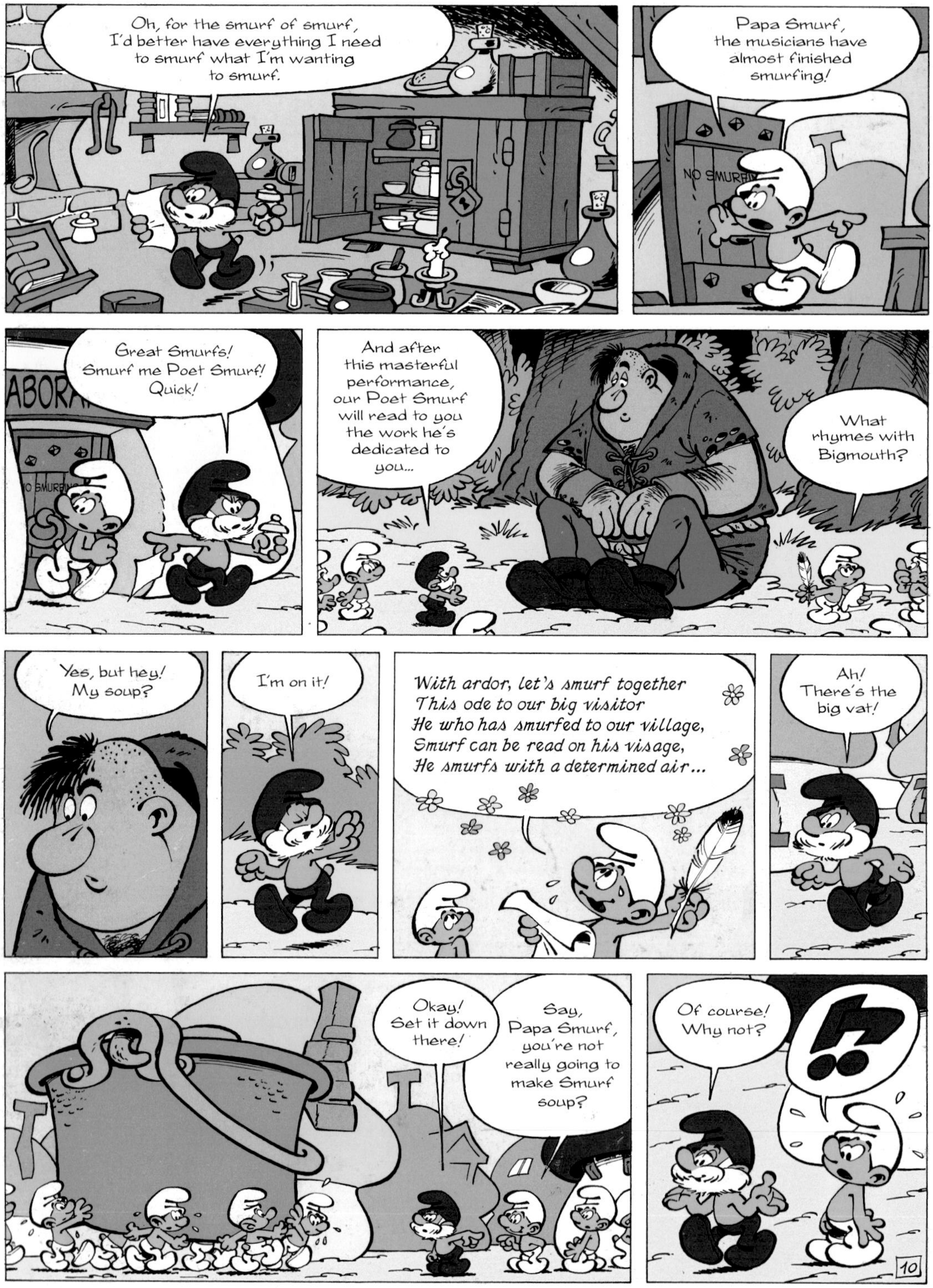
Oh, for the smurf of smurf, I'd better have everything I need to smurf what I'm wanting to smurf.
Papa Smurf, the musicians have almost finished smurfing!
NO SMURFI
ABORA
NO SMURFIN
Great Smurfs! Smurf me Poet Smurf! Quick!
And after this masterful performance, our Poet Smurf will read to you the work he's dedicated to you...
What rhymes with Bigmouth?
Yes, but hey! My soup?
I'm on it!
With ardor, let's smurf together
This ode to our big visitor
He who has smurfed to our village,
Smurf can be read on his visage,
He smurfs with a determined air...
Ah! There's the big vat!
Okay! Set it down there!
Say, Papa Smurf, you're not really going to make Smurf soup?
Of course! Why not?
10

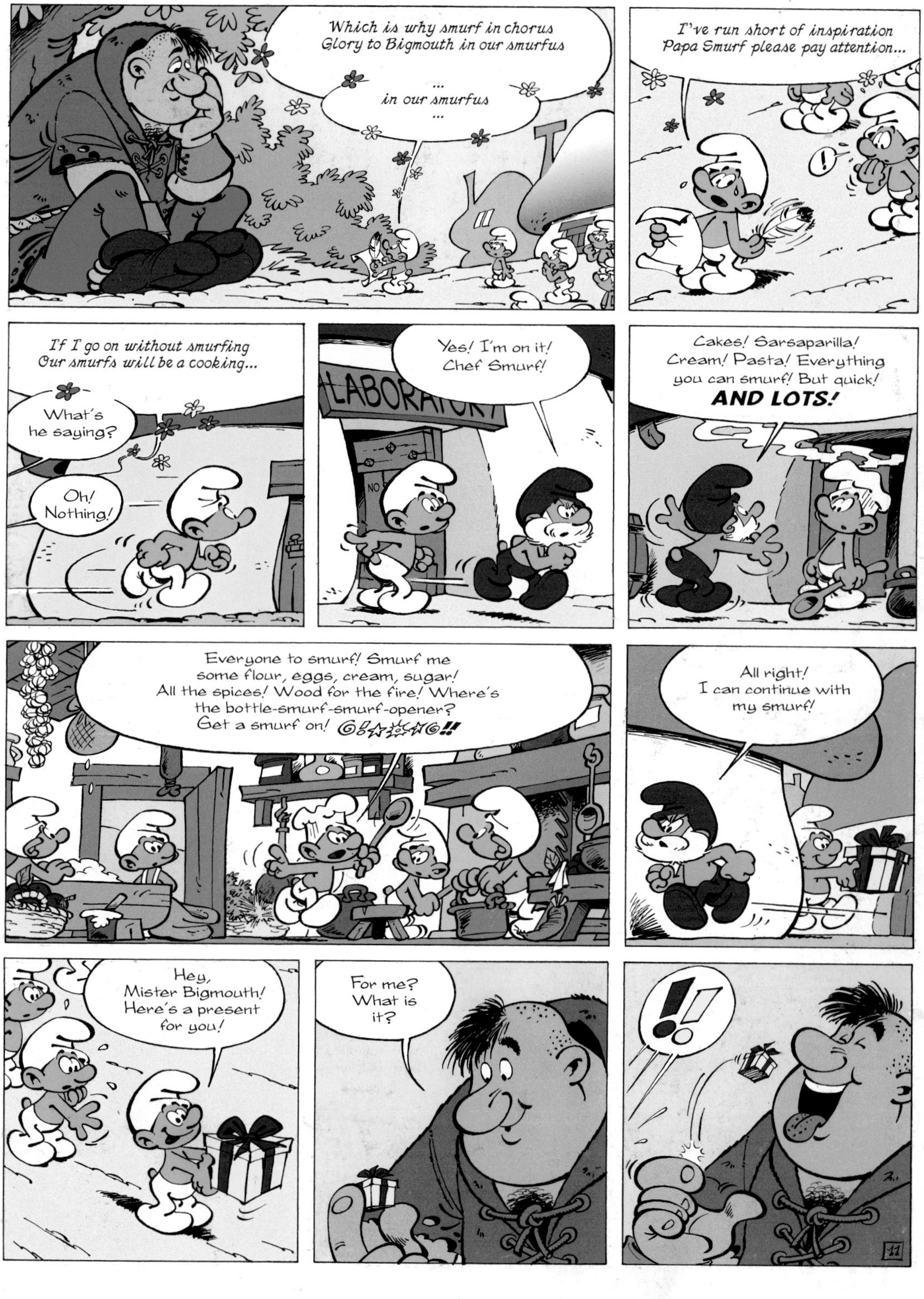
Which is why smurf in chorus
Glory to Bigmouth in our smurfus
... in our smurfus ...
I've run short of inspiration
Papa Smurf please pay attention...
If I go on without smurfing
Our smurfs will be a cooking...
What's he saying?
Oh! Nothing!
Yes! I'm on it! Chef Smurf!
LABORATORY
Cakes! Sarsaparilla! Cream! Pasta! Everything you can smurf! But quick!
AND LOTS!
Everyone to smurf! Smurf me some flour, eggs, cream, sugar! All the spices! Wood for the fire! Where's the bottle-smurf-smurf-opener? Get a smurf on!
All right! I can continue with my smurf!
Hey, Mister Bigmouth! Here's a present for you!
For me? What is it?
11

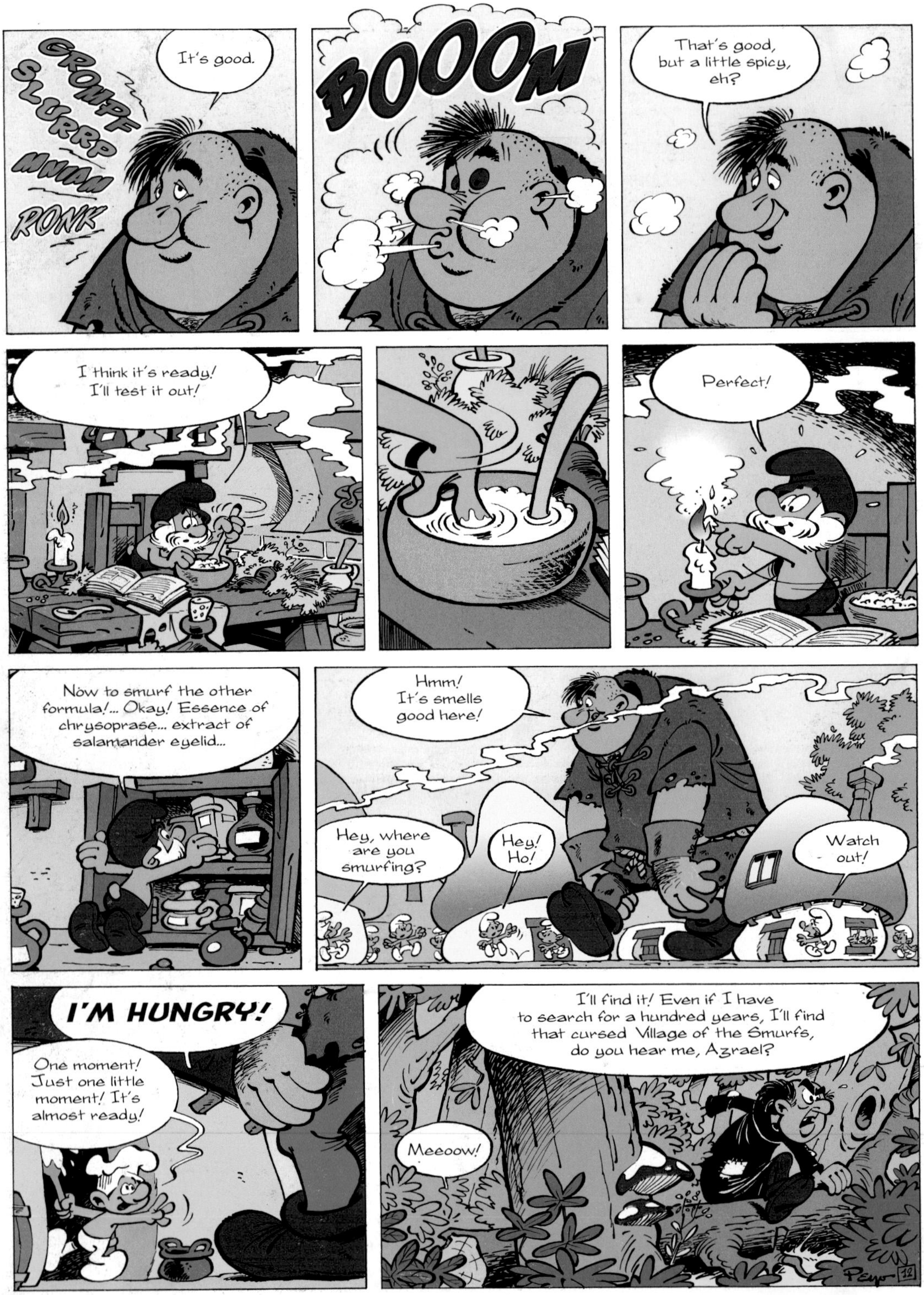
GROMPF
SLURRP
MNIAM
RONK
It's good.
BOOOM
That's good, but a little spicy, eh?
I think it's ready! I'll test it out!
Perfect!
Now to smurf the other formula!... Okay! Essence of chrysoprase... extract of salamander eyelid...
Hmm! It's smells good here!
Hey, where are you smurfing?
Hey! Ho!
Watch out!
I'M HUNGRY!
One moment! Just one little moment! It's almost ready!
I'll find it! Even if I have to search for a hundred years, I'll find that cursed Village of the Smurfs, do you hear me, Azrael?
Meeoow!

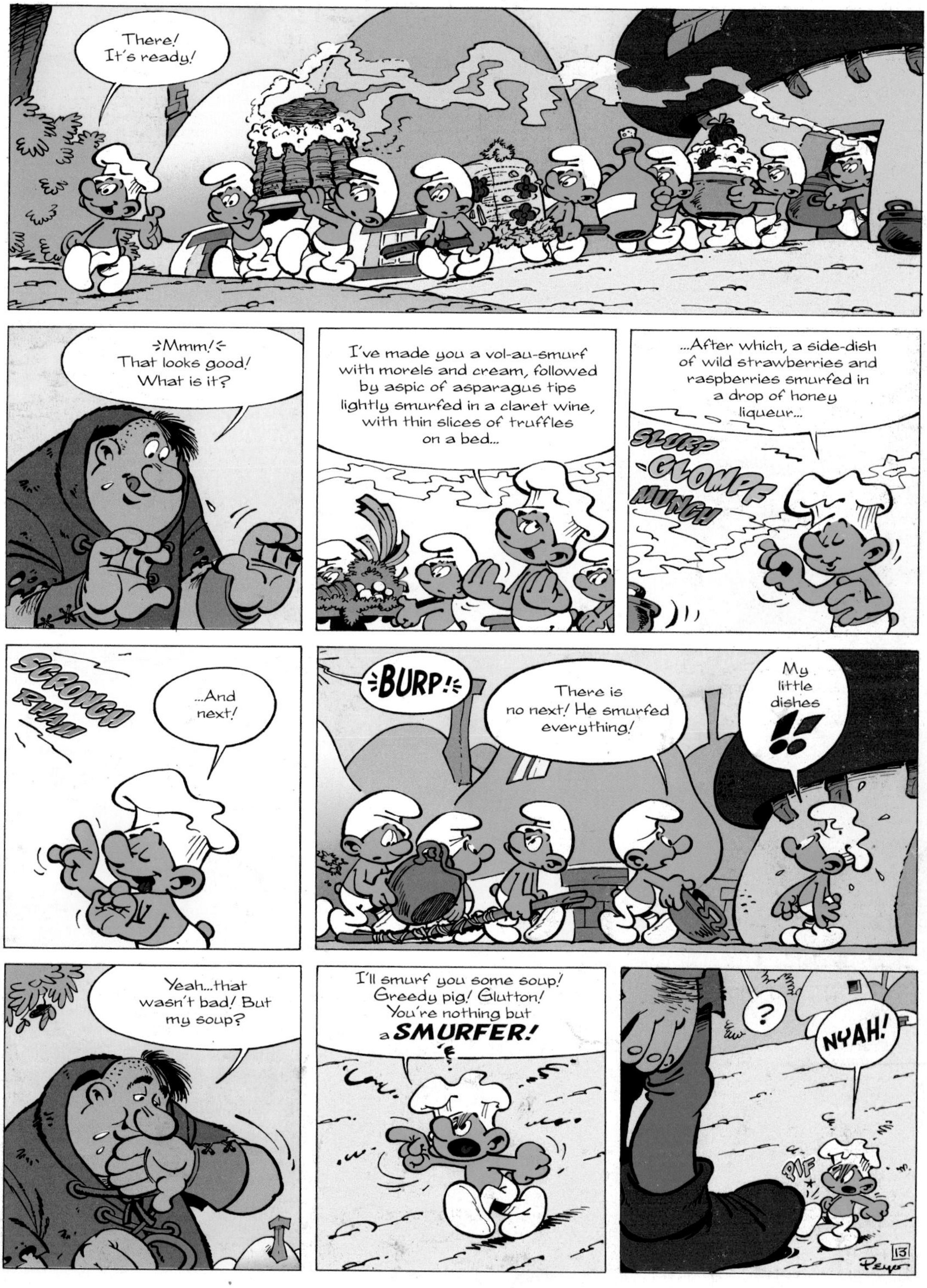
There! It's ready!
Mmm! That looks good! What is it?
I've made you a vol-au-smurf with morels and cream, followed by aspic of asparagus tips lightly smurfed in a claret wine, with thin slices of truffles on a bed...
...After which, a side-dish of wild strawberries and raspberries smurfed in a drop of honey liqueur...
SLURP
GLOMPF
MUNCH
SCRONCH
RHAM
...And next!
BURP!
There is no next! He smurfed everything!
My little dishes
Yeah...that wasn't bad! But my soup?
I'll smurf you some soup! Greedy pig! Glutton! You're nothing but a SMURFER!
?
NYAH!
PIF
13
Peyo

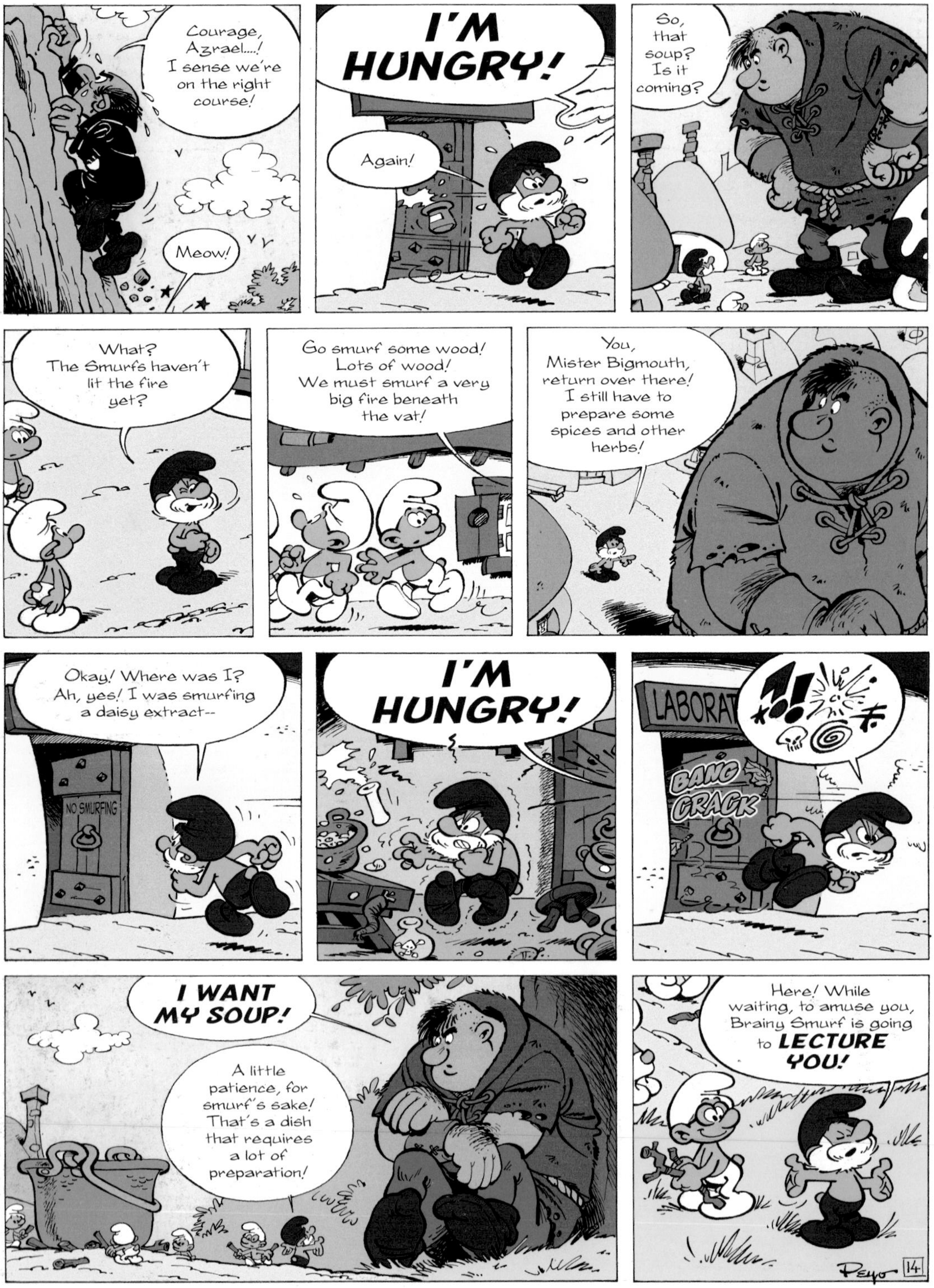
Courage, Azrael....! I sense we're on the right course!
Meow!
I'M HUNGRY!
Again!
So, that soup? Is it coming?
What? The Smurfs haven't lit the fire yet?
Go smurf some wood! Lots of wood! We must smurf a very big fire beneath the vat!
You, Mister Bigmouth, return over there! I still have to prepare some spices and other herbs!
Okay! Where was I? Ah, yes! I was smurfing a daisy extract--
NO SMURFING
I'M HUNGRY!
LABORAT
BANG
CRACK
I WANT MY SOUP!
A little patience, for smurf's sake! That's a dish that requires a lot of preparation!
Here! While waiting, to amuse you, Brainy Smurf is going to LECTURE YOU!
Peyo
14

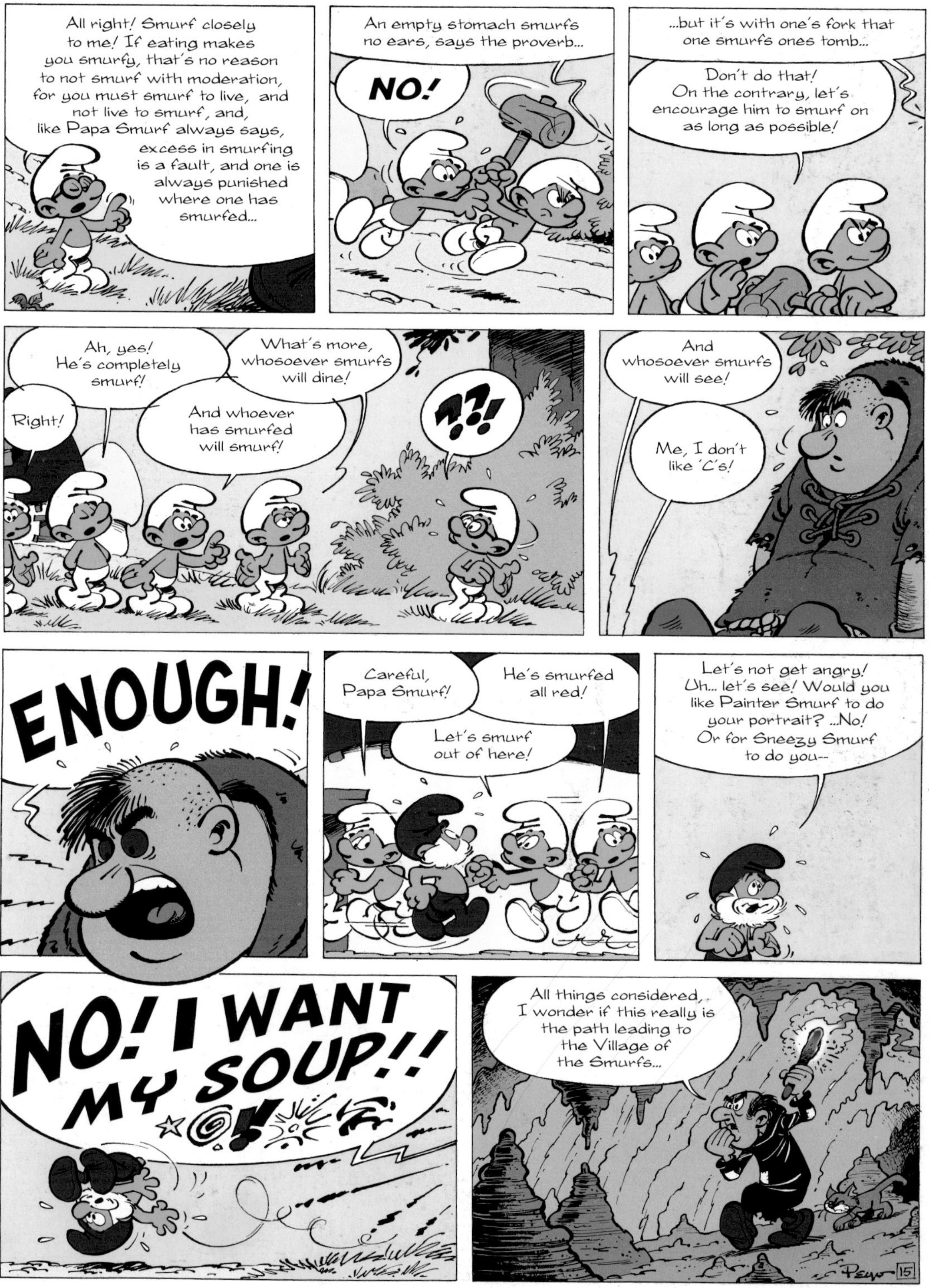
All right! Smurf closely to me! If eating makes you smurfy, that's no reason to not smurf with moderation, for you must smurf to live, and not live to smurf, and, like Papa Smurf always says, excess in smurfing is a fault, and one is always punished where one has smurfed...
An empty stomach smurfs no ears, says the proverb...
NO!
...but it's with one's fork that one smurfs ones tomb...
Don't do that! On the contrary, let's encourage him to smurf on as long as possible!
Ah, yes! He's completely smurf!
What's more, whosoever smurfs will dine!
Right!
And whoever has smurfed will smurf!
??!
And whosoever smurfs will see!
Me, I don't like 'C's!
ENOUGH!
Careful, Papa Smurf!
He's smurfed all red!
Let's smurf out of here!
Let's not get angry! Uh... let's see! Would you like Painter Smurf to do your portrait? ...No! Or for Sneezy Smurf to do you--
NO! I WANT MY SOUP!!
All things considered, I wonder if this really is the path leading to the Village of the Smurfs...
Peyo
15

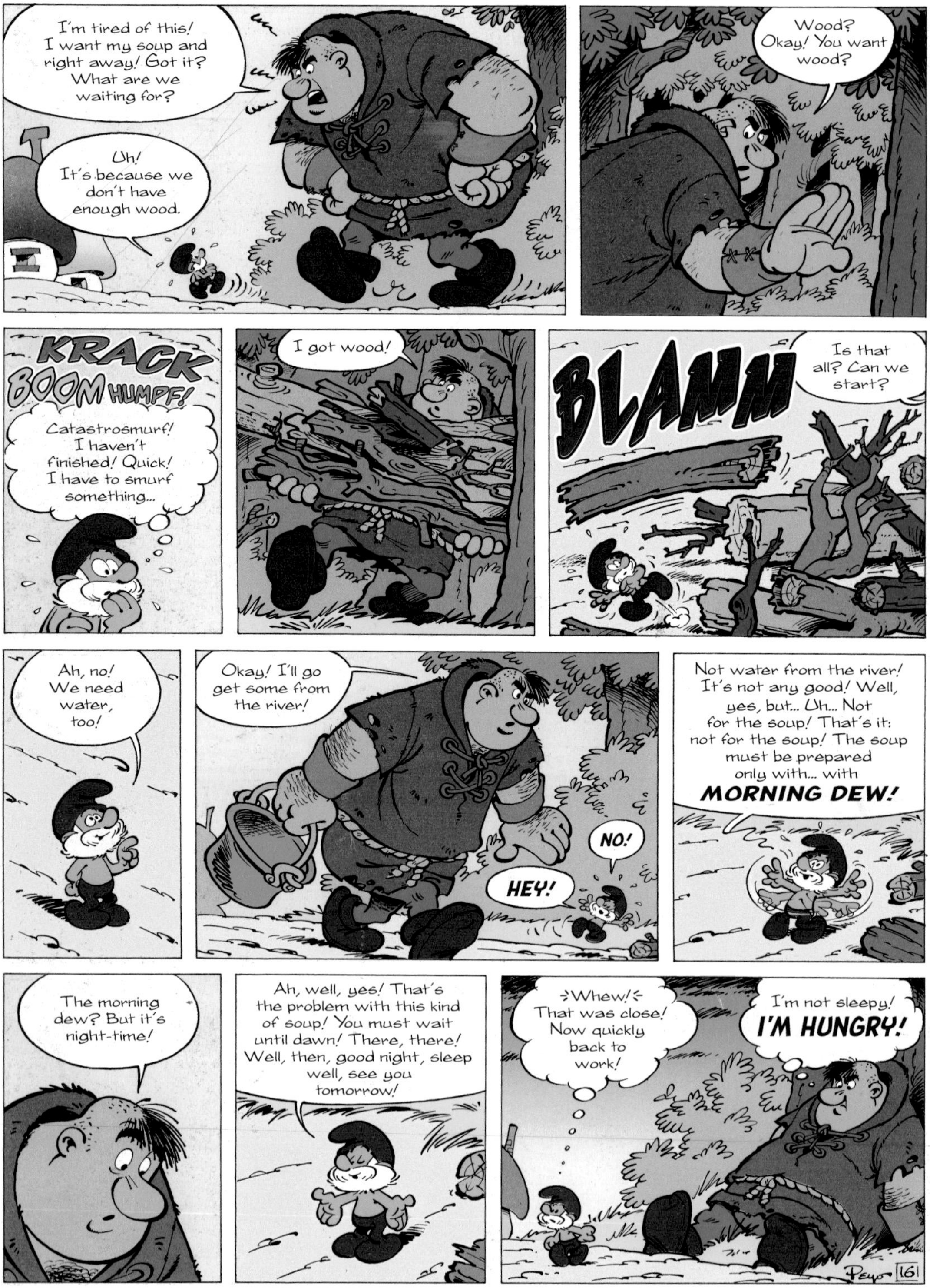
I'm tired of this! I want my soup and right away! Got it? What are we waiting for?
Uh! It's because we don't have enough wood.
Wood? Okay! You want wood?
KRACK
BOOM HUMPF!
Catastrosmurf! I haven't finished! Quick! I have to smurf something...
I got wood!
BLAMM
Is that all? Can we start?
Ah, no! We need water, too!
Okay! I'll go get some from the river!
NO!
HEY!
Not water from the river! It's not any good! Well, yes, but... Uh... Not for the soup! That's it: not for the soup! The soup must be prepared only with... with MORNING DEW!
The morning dew? But it's night-time!
Ah, well, yes! That's the problem with this kind of soup! You must wait until dawn! There, there! Well, then, good night, sleep well, see you tomorrow!
Whew! That was close! Now quickly back to work!
I'm not sleepy! I'M HUNGRY!
Peyo
16

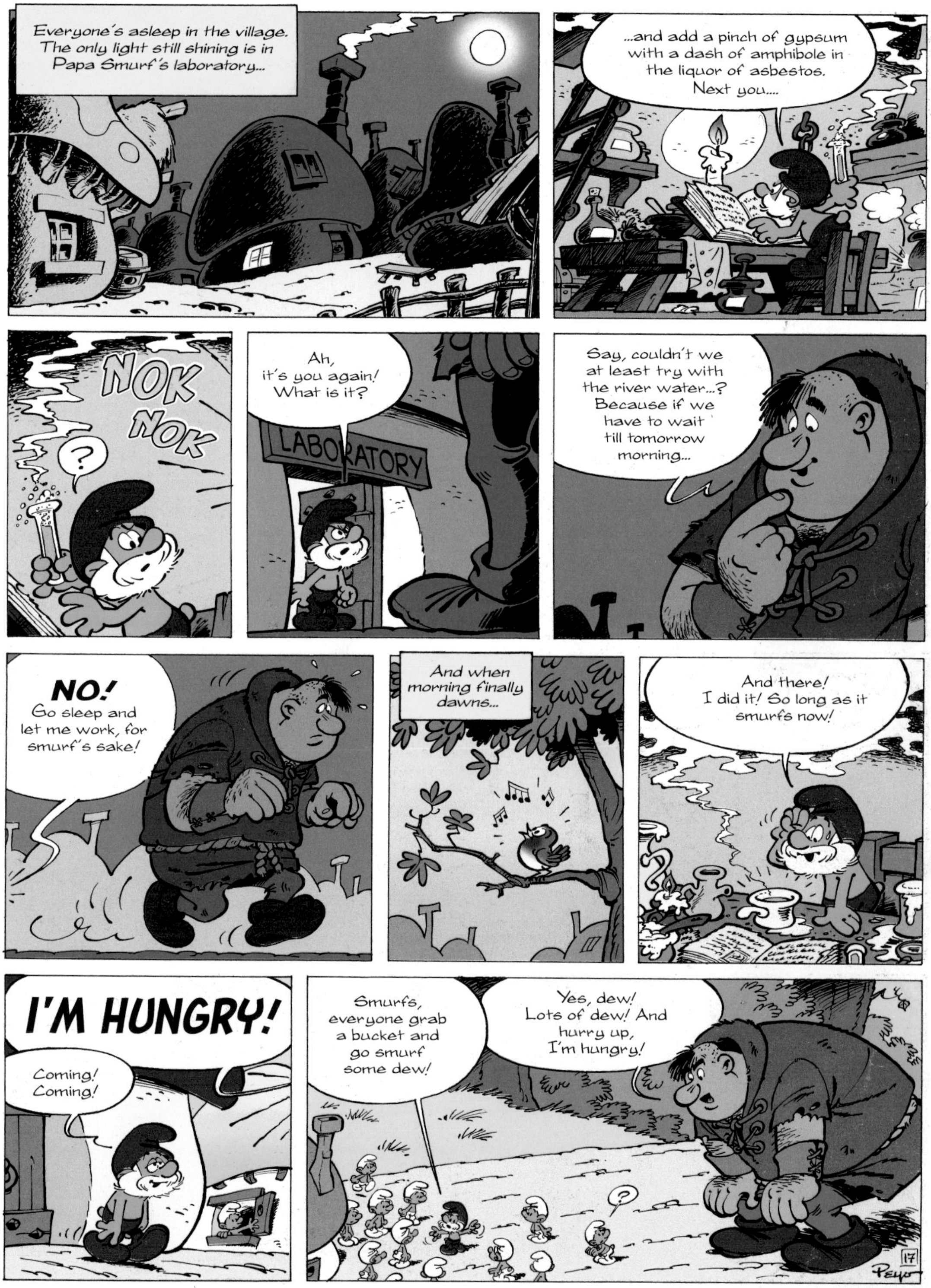

Everyone's asleep in the village. The only light still shining is in Papa Smurf's laboratory...
...and add a pinch of gypsum with a dash of amphibole in the liquor of asbestos. Next you....
NOK NOK
?
Ah, it's you again! What is it?
LABORATORY
Say, couldn't we at least try with the river water...? Because if we have to wait till tomorrow morning...
NO! Go sleep and let me work, for smurf's sake!
And when morning finally dawns...
And there! I did it! So long as it smurfs now!
I'M HUNGRY!
Coming! Coming!
Smurfs, everyone grab a bucket and go smurf some dew!
Yes, dew! Lots of dew! And hurry up, I'm hungry!
?
17

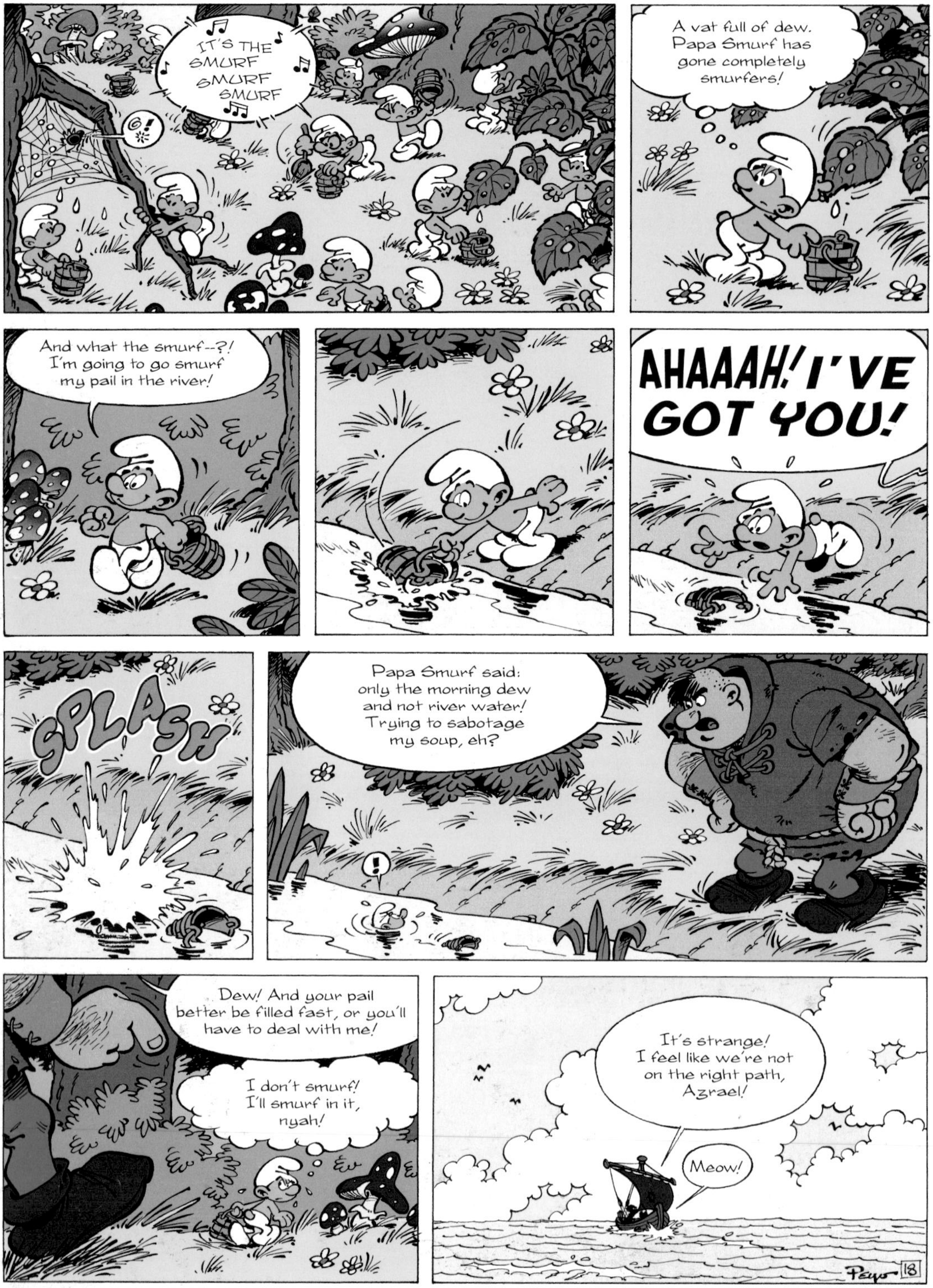

IT'S THE SMURF SMURF SMURF
A vat full of dew. Papa Smurf has gone completely smurfers!
And what the smurf--?! I'm going to go smurf my pail in the river!
AHAAAH! I'VE GOT YOU!
SPLASH
Papa Smurf said: only the morning dew and not river water! Trying to sabotage my soup, eh?
Dew! And your pail better be filled fast, or you'll have to deal with me!
I don't smurf! I'll smurf in it, nyah!
It's strange! I feel like we're not on the right path, Azrael!
Meow!

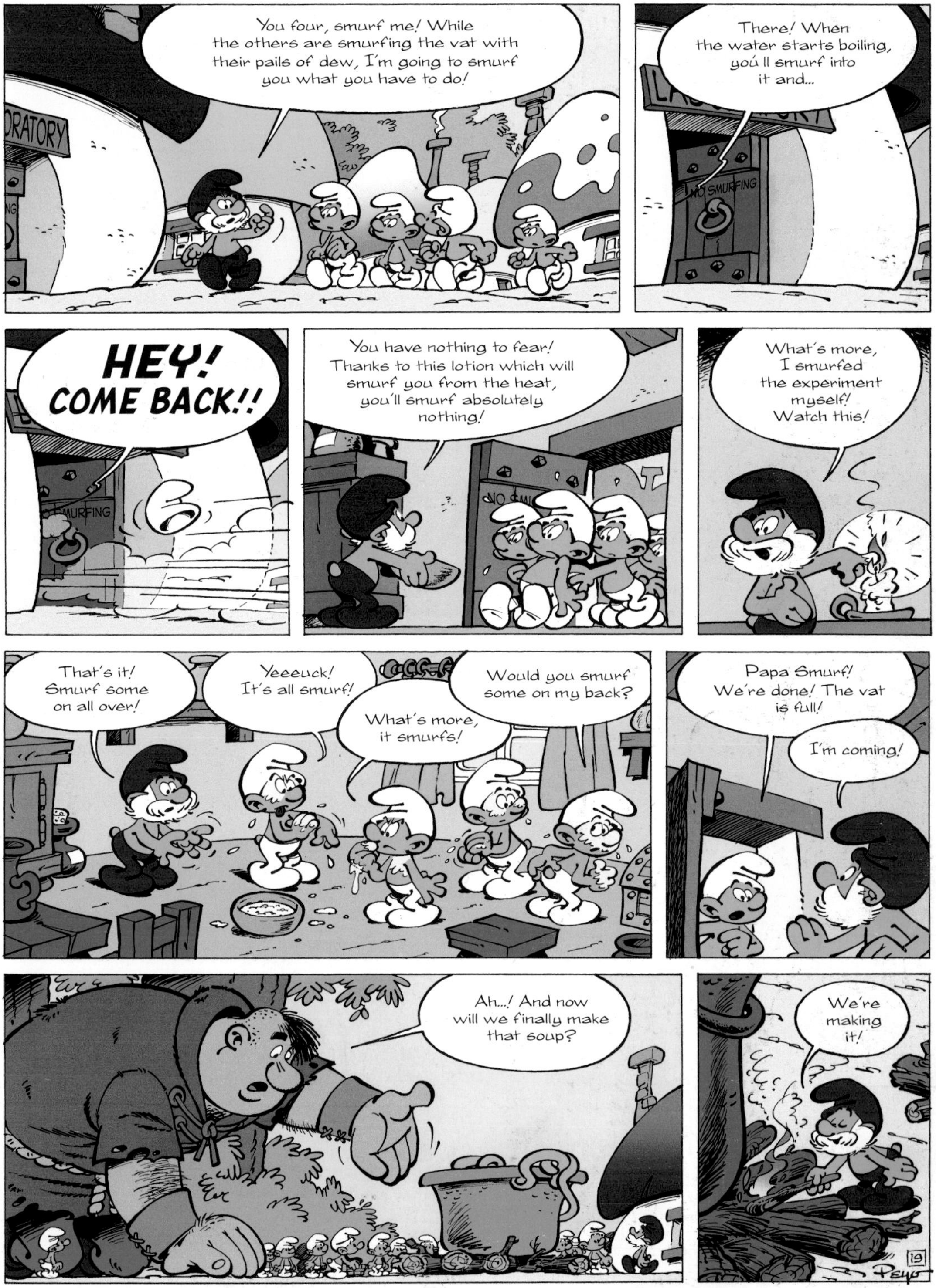
You four, smurf me! While the others are smurfing the vat with their pails of dew, I'm going to smurf you what you have to do!
There! When the water starts boiling, you'll smurf into it and...
NO SMURFING
HEY! COME BACK!!
You have nothing to fear! Thanks to this lotion which will smurf you from the heat, you'll smurf absolutely nothing!
What's more, I smurfed the experiment myself! Watch this!
That's it! Smurf some on all over!
Yeeeuck! It's all smurf!
What's more, it smurfs!
Would you smurf some on my back?
Papa Smurf! We're done! The vat is full!
I'm coming!
Ah...! And now will we finally make that soup?
We're making it!
19
Peyo

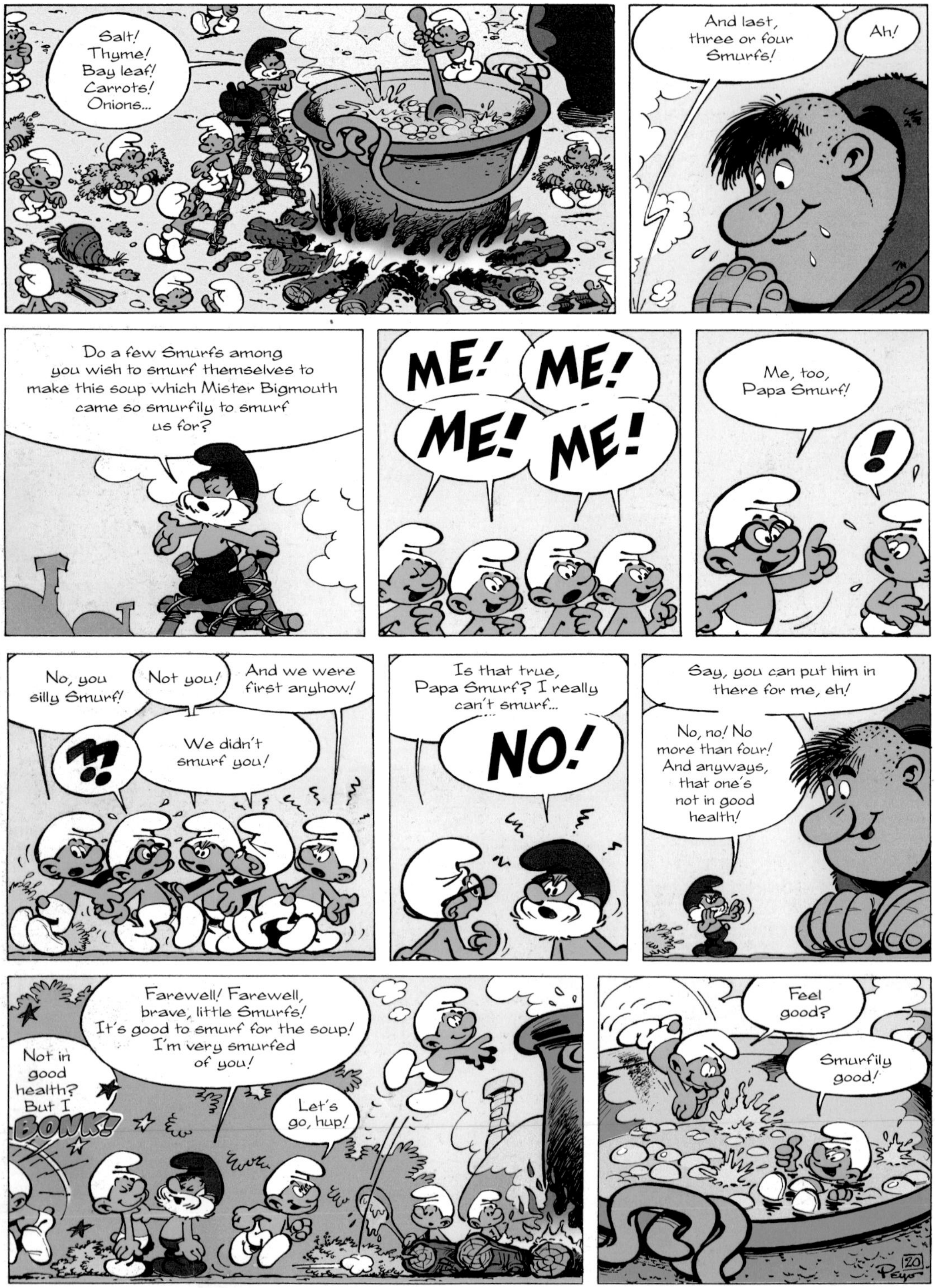

Salt! Thyme! Bay leaf! Carrots! Onions...
And last, three or four Smurfs!
Ah!
Do a few Smurfs among you wish to smurf themselves to make this soup which Mister Bigmouth came so smurfily to smurf us for?
ME!
ME!
ME!
ME!
Me, too, Papa Smurf!
!
No, you silly Smurf!
Not you!
And we were first anyhow!
We didn't smurf you!
?!
Is that true, Papa Smurf? I really can't smurf...
NO!
Say, you can put him in there for me, eh!
No, no! No more than four! And anyways, that one's not in good health!
Farewell! Farewell, brave, little Smurfs! It's good to smurf for the soup! I'm very smurfed of you!
Not in good health? But I
BONK!
Let's go, hup!
Feel good?
Smurfily good!
20
Peyo

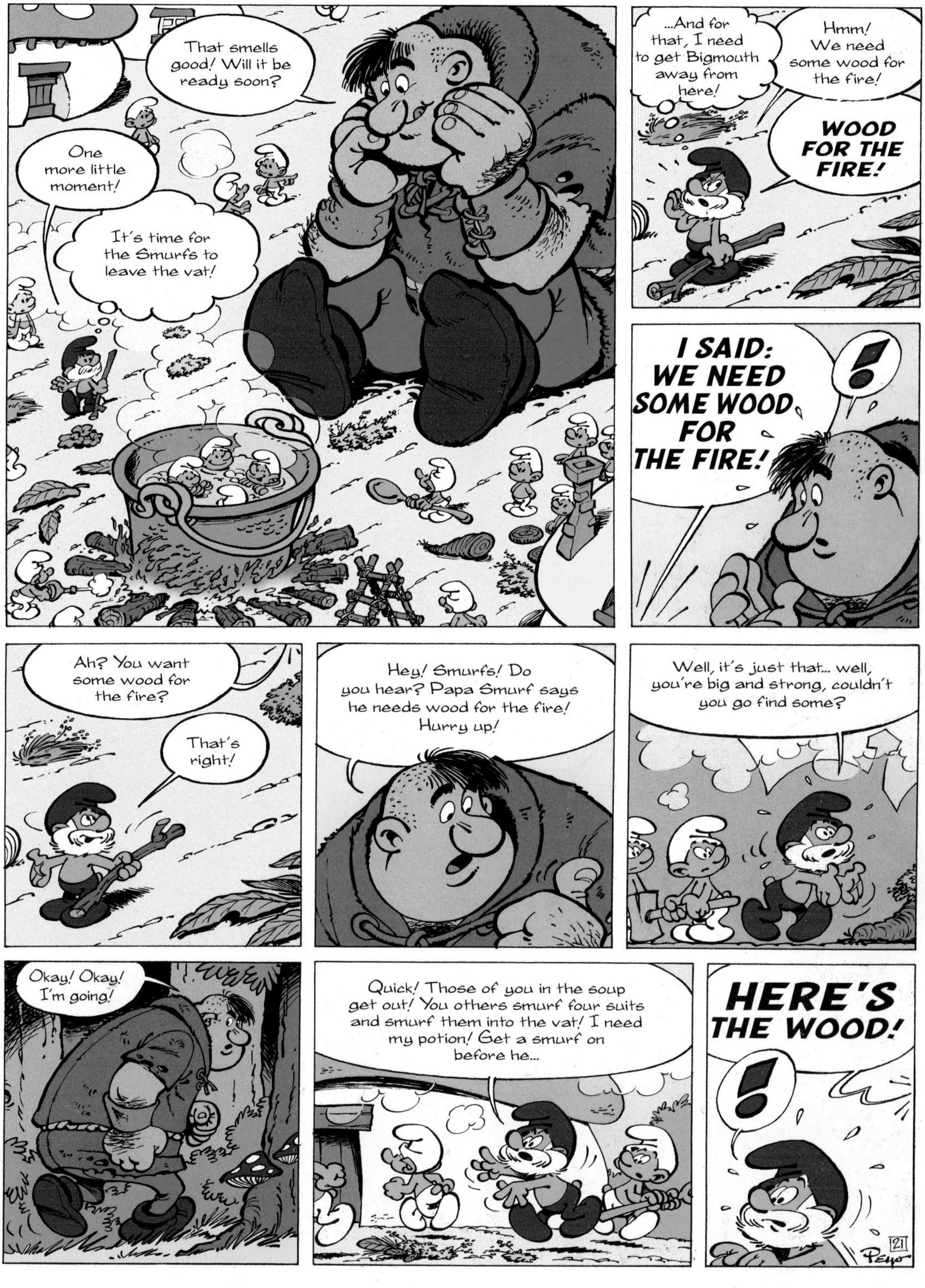
That smells good! Will it be ready soon?
One more little moment!
It's time for the Smurfs to leave the vat!
...And for that, I need to get Bigmouth away from here!
Hmm! We need some wood for the fire!
WOOD FOR THE FIRE!
I SAID: WE NEED SOME WOOD FOR THE FIRE!
!
Ah? You want some wood for the fire?
That's right!
Hey! Smurfs! Do you hear? Papa Smurf says he needs wood for the fire! Hurry up!
Well, it's just that... well, you're big and strong, couldn't you go find some?
Okay! Okay! I'm going!
Quick! Those of you in the soup get out! You others smurf four suits and smurf them into the vat! I need my potion! Get a smurf on before he...
HERE'S THE WOOD!
!
21
Peyo

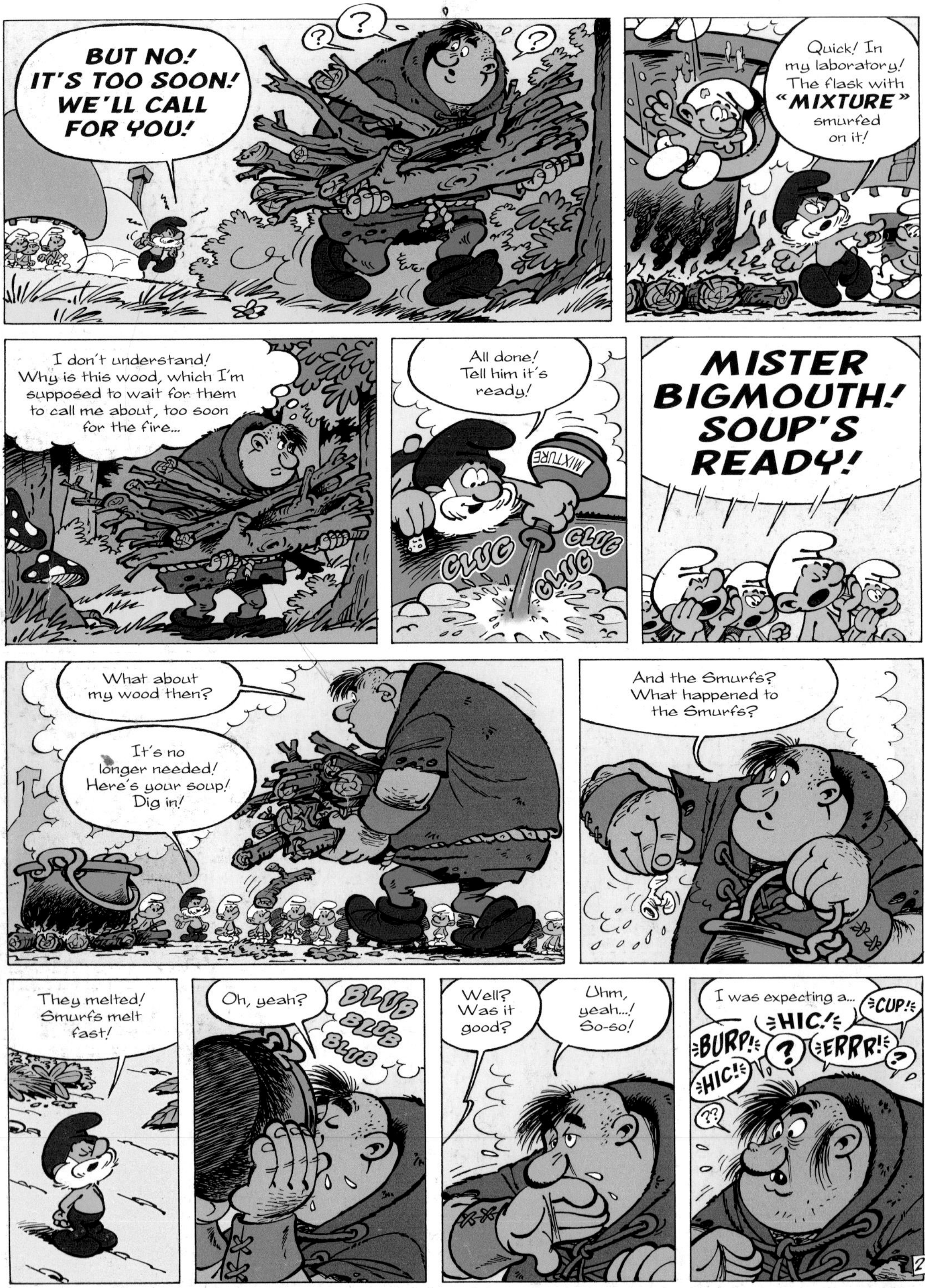

BUT NO! IT'S TOO SOON! WE'LL CALL FOR YOU!
?
?
?
Quick! In my laboratory! The flask with «MIXTURE» smurfed on it!
I don't understand! Why is this wood, which I'm supposed to wait for them to call me about, too soon for the fire...
All done! Tell him it's ready!
MIXTURE
GLUG
GLUG
GLUG
MISTER BIGMOUTH! SOUP'S READY!
What about my wood then?
It's no longer needed! Here's your soup! Dig in!
And the Smurfs? What happened to the Smurfs?
They melted! Smurfs melt fast!
Oh, yeah?
BLUB
BLUB
BLUB
Well? Was it good?
Uhm, yeah...! So-so!
I was expecting a...
CUP!
HIC!
BURP!
?
ERRR!
?
HIC!
??
22

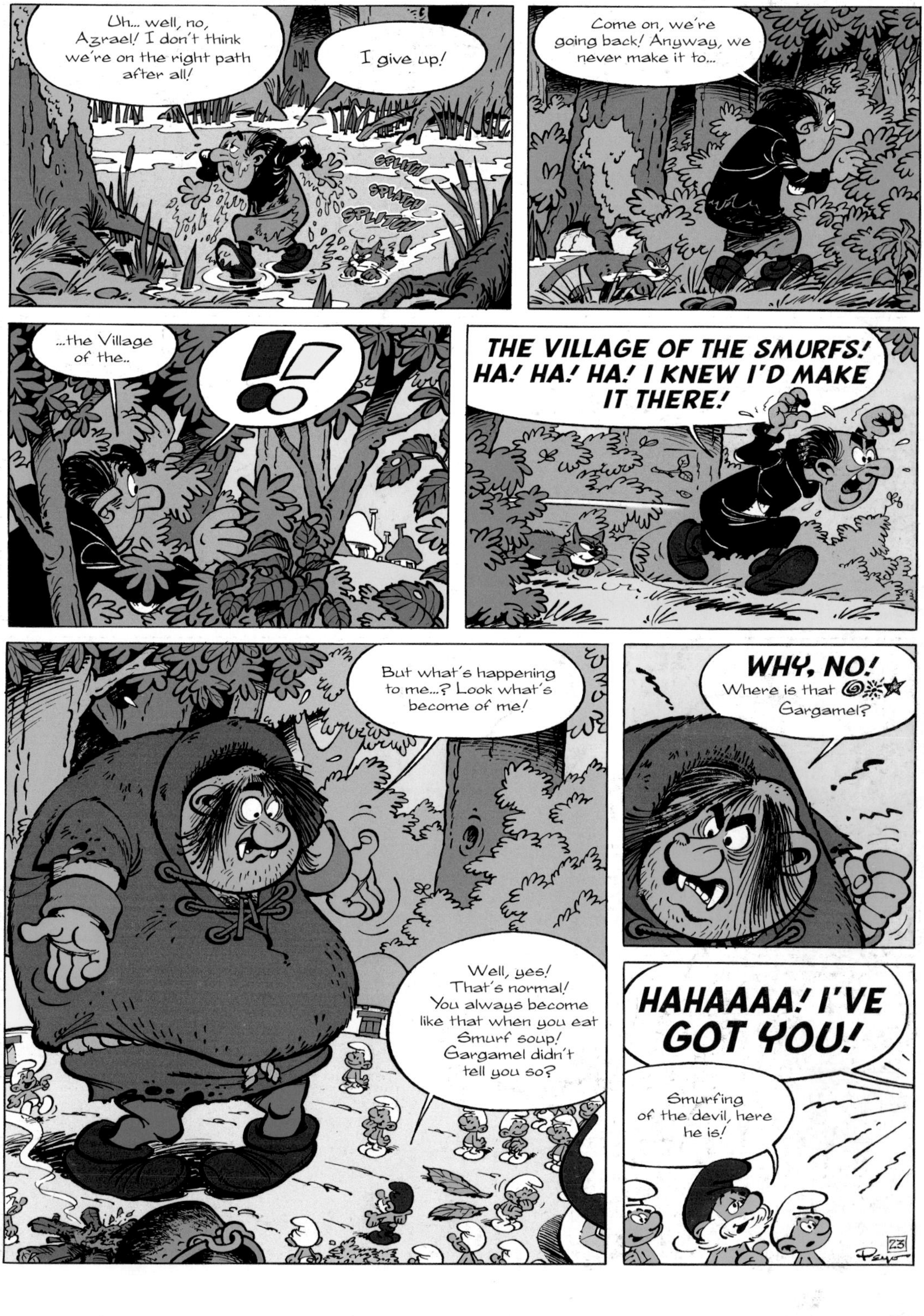
Uh... well, no, Azrael! I don't think we're on the right path after all!
I give up!
SPLITCH
SPLATCH
SPLITCH
Come on, we're going back! Anyway, we never make it to...
...the Village of the..
THE VILLAGE OF THE SMURFS! HA! HA! HA! I KNEW I'D MAKE IT THERE!
But what's happening to me...? Look what's become of me!
Well, yes! That's normal! You always become like that when you eat Smurf soup! Gargamel didn't tell you so?
WHY, NO! Where is that Gargamel?
HAHAAAA! I'VE GOT YOU!
Smurfing of the devil, here he is!
23
Peyo

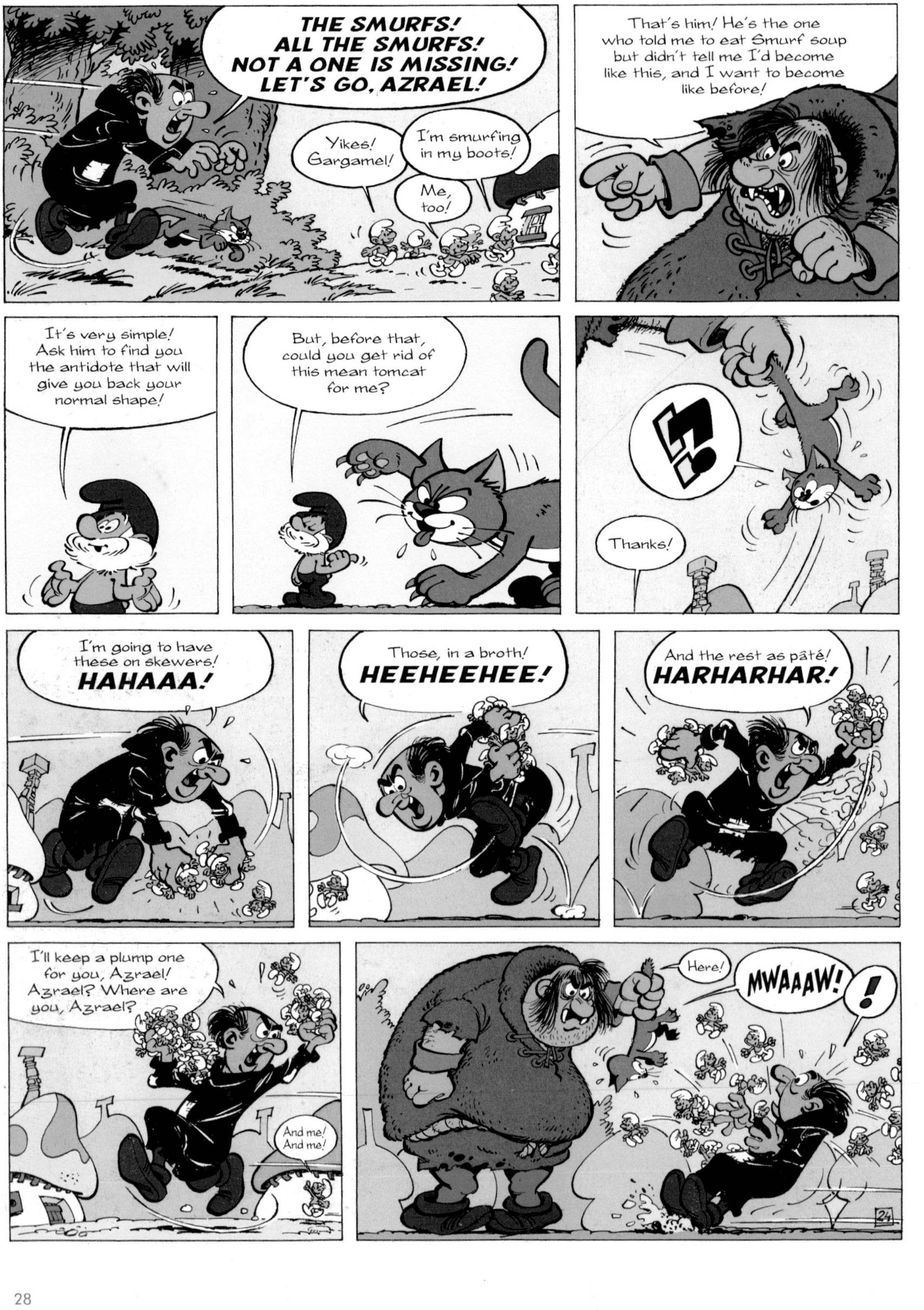
THE SMURFS! ALL THE SMURFS! NOT A ONE IS MISSING! LET'S GO, AZRAEL!
Yikes! Gargamel!
I'm smurfing in my boots!
Me, too!
That's him! He's the one who told me to eat Smurf soup but didn't tell me I'd become like this, and I want to become like before!
It's very simple! Ask him to find you the antidote that will give you back your normal shape!
But, before that, could you get rid of this mean tomcat for me?
!?
Thanks!
I'm going to have these on skewers! HAHAAA!
Those, in a broth! HEEHEEHEE!
And the rest as pâté! HARHARHAR!
I'll keep a plump one for you, Azrael! Azrael? Where are you, Azrael?
And me! And me!
Here!
MWAAAW!
!
24

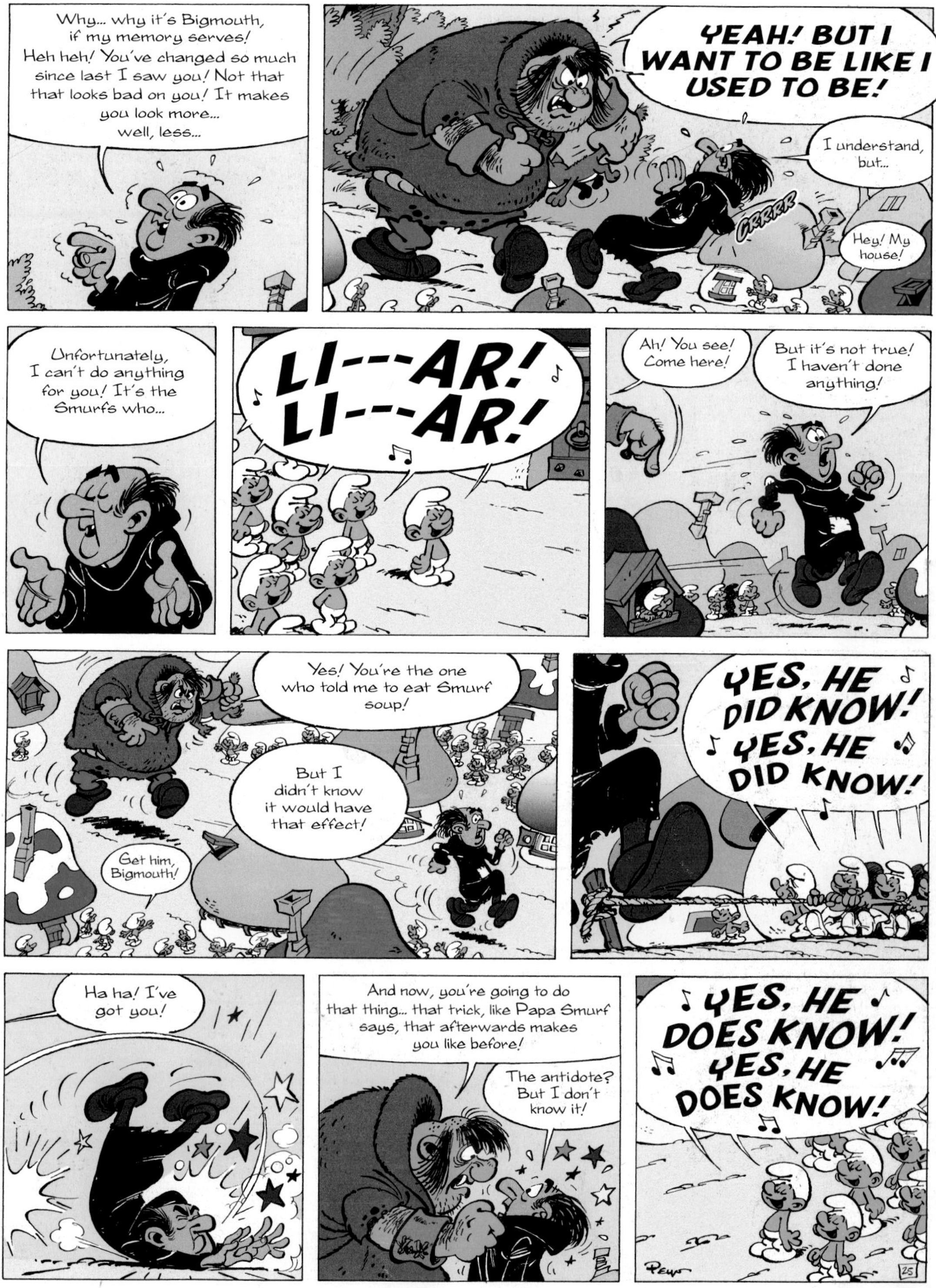

Why... why it's Bigmouth, if my memory serves! Heh heh! You've changed so much since last I saw you! Not that that looks bad on you! It makes you look more... well, less...
YEAH! BUT I WANT TO BE LIKE I USED TO BE!
I understand, but...
CRRRR
Hey! My house!
Unfortunately, I can't do anything for you! It's the Smurfs who...
LI---AR! LI---AR!
Ah! You see! Come here!
But it's not true! I haven't done anything!
Yes! You're the one who told me to eat Smurf soup!
But I didn't know it would have that effect!
Get him, Bigmouth!
YES, HE DID KNOW! YES, HE DID KNOW!
Ha ha! I've got you!
And now, you're going to do that thing... that trick, like Papa Smurf says, that afterwards makes you like before!
The antidote? But I don't know it!
YES, HE DOES KNOW! YES, HE DOES KNOW!
25

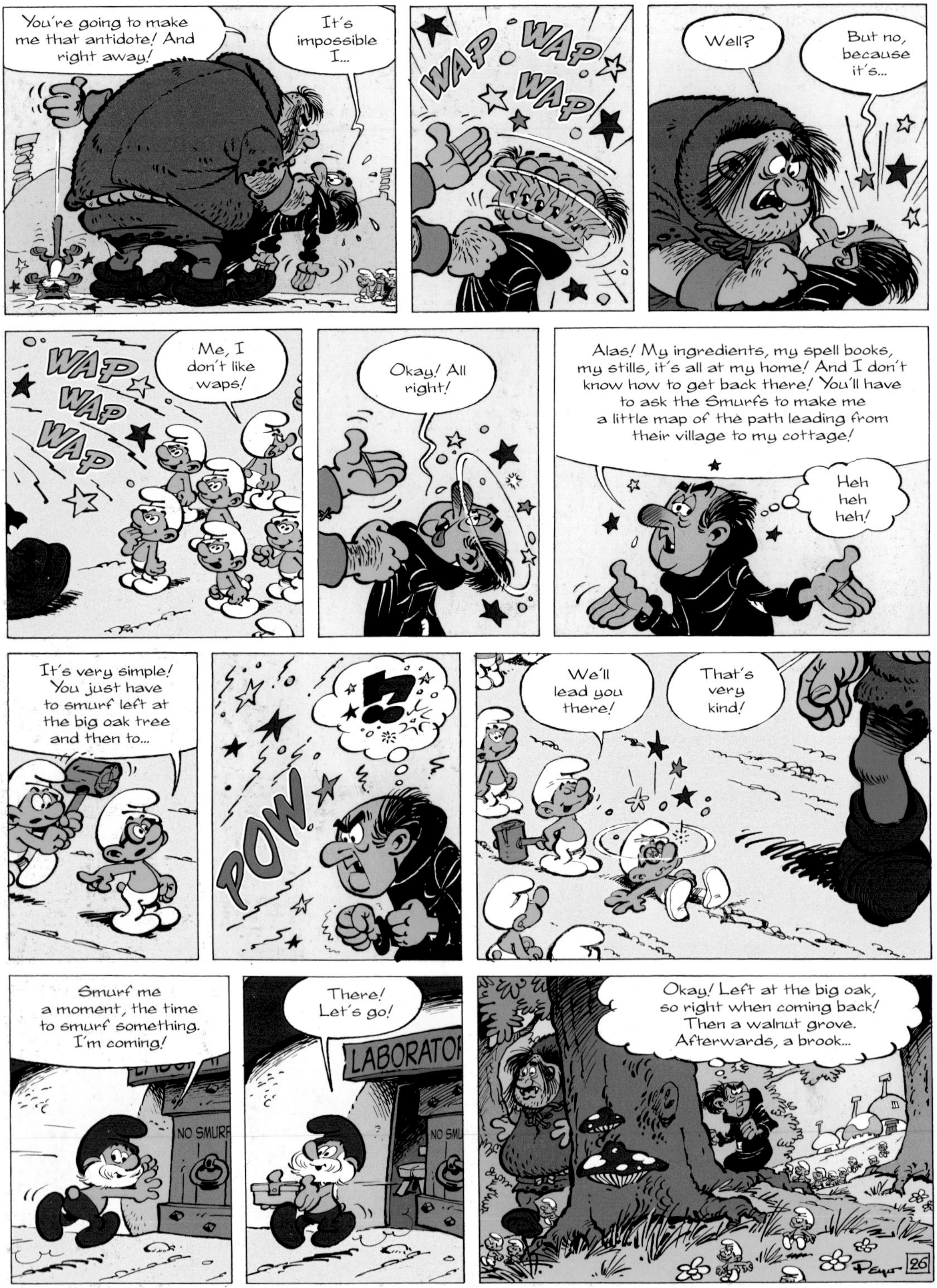
You're going to make me that antidote! And right away!
It's impossible I...
WAP WAP WAP
Well?
But no, because it's...
WAP WAP WAP
Me, I don't like waps!
Okay! All right!
Alas! My ingredients, my spell books, my stills, it's all at my home! And I don't know how to get back there! You'll have to ask the Smurfs to make me a little map of the path leading from their village to my cottage!
Heh heh heh!
It's very simple! You just have to smurf left at the big oak tree and then to...
POW
We'll lead you there!
That's very kind!
Smurf me a moment, the time to smurf something. I'm coming!
NO SMURF
There! Let's go!
LABORATOR
NO SMU
Okay! Left at the big oak, so right when coming back! Then a walnut grove. Afterwards, a brook...
26

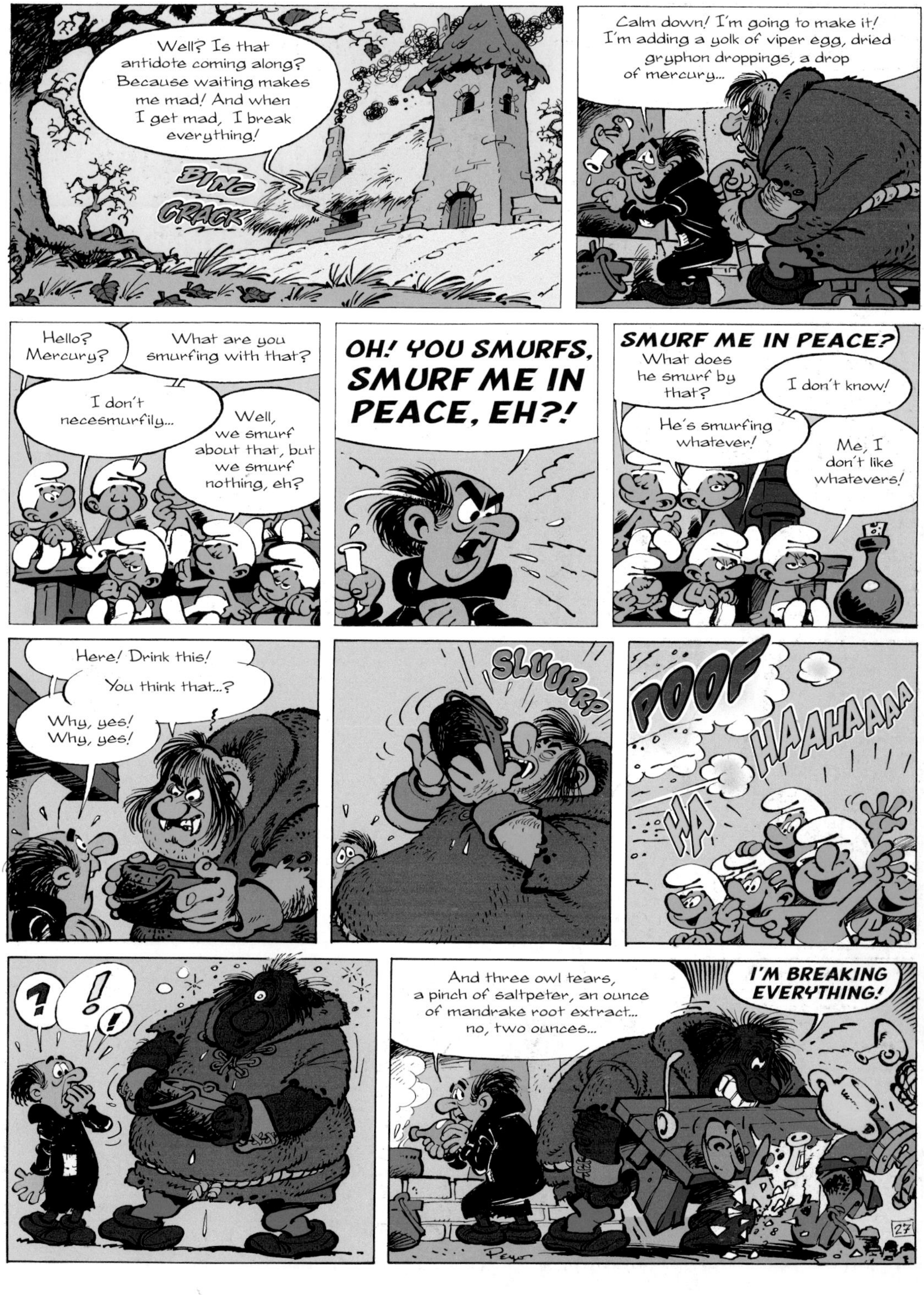
Well? Is that antidote coming along? Because waiting makes me mad! And when I get mad, I break everything!
BING
CRACK
Calm down! I'm going to make it! I'm adding a yolk of viper egg, dried gryphon droppings, a drop of mercury...
Hello? Mercury?
What are you smurfing with that?
I don't necesmurfily...
Well, we smurf about that, but we smurf nothing, eh?
OH! YOU SMURFS, SMURF ME IN PEACE, EH?!
SMURF ME IN PEACE?
What does he smurf by that?
I don't know!
He's smurfing whatever!
Me, I don't like whatevers!
Here! Drink this!
You think that...?
Why, yes! Why, yes!
SLUURRP
POOF
HAAHAAAA
HA
?
!
!
And three owl tears, a pinch of saltpeter, an ounce of mandrake root extract... no, two ounces...
I'M BREAKING EVERYTHING!
27
Peyo

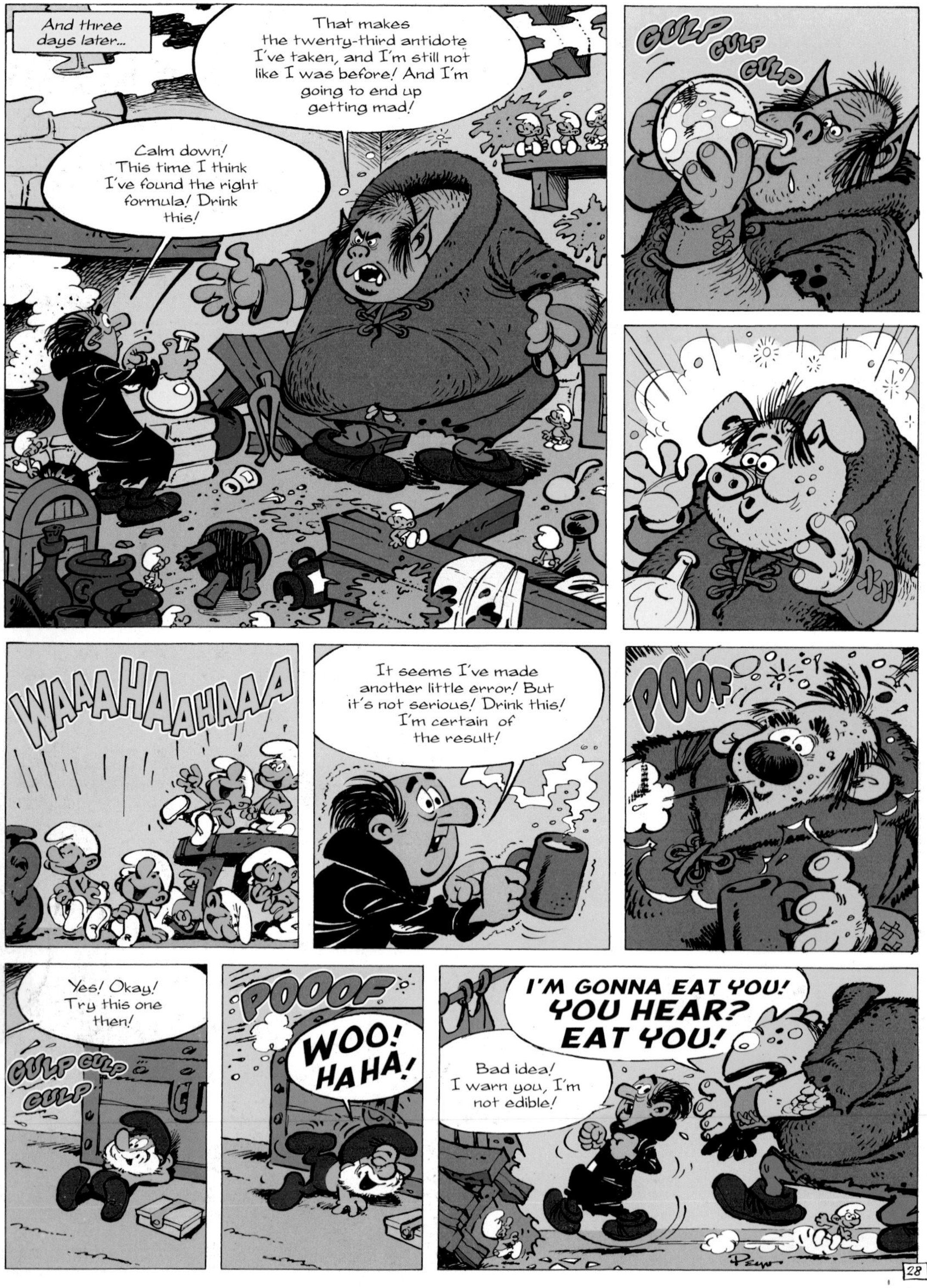
And three days later...
That makes the twenty-third antidote I've taken, and I'm still not like I was before! And I'm going to end up getting mad!
Calm down! This time I think I've found the right formula! Drink this!
GULP GULP GULP
WAAAHAAAHAAA
It seems I've made another little error! But it's not serious! Drink this! I'm certain of the result!
POOF
Yes! Okay! Try this one then!
GULP GULP GULP
POOOF
WOO! HAHA!
I'M GONNA EAT YOU! YOU HEAR? EAT YOU!
Bad idea! I warn you, I'm not edible!
28

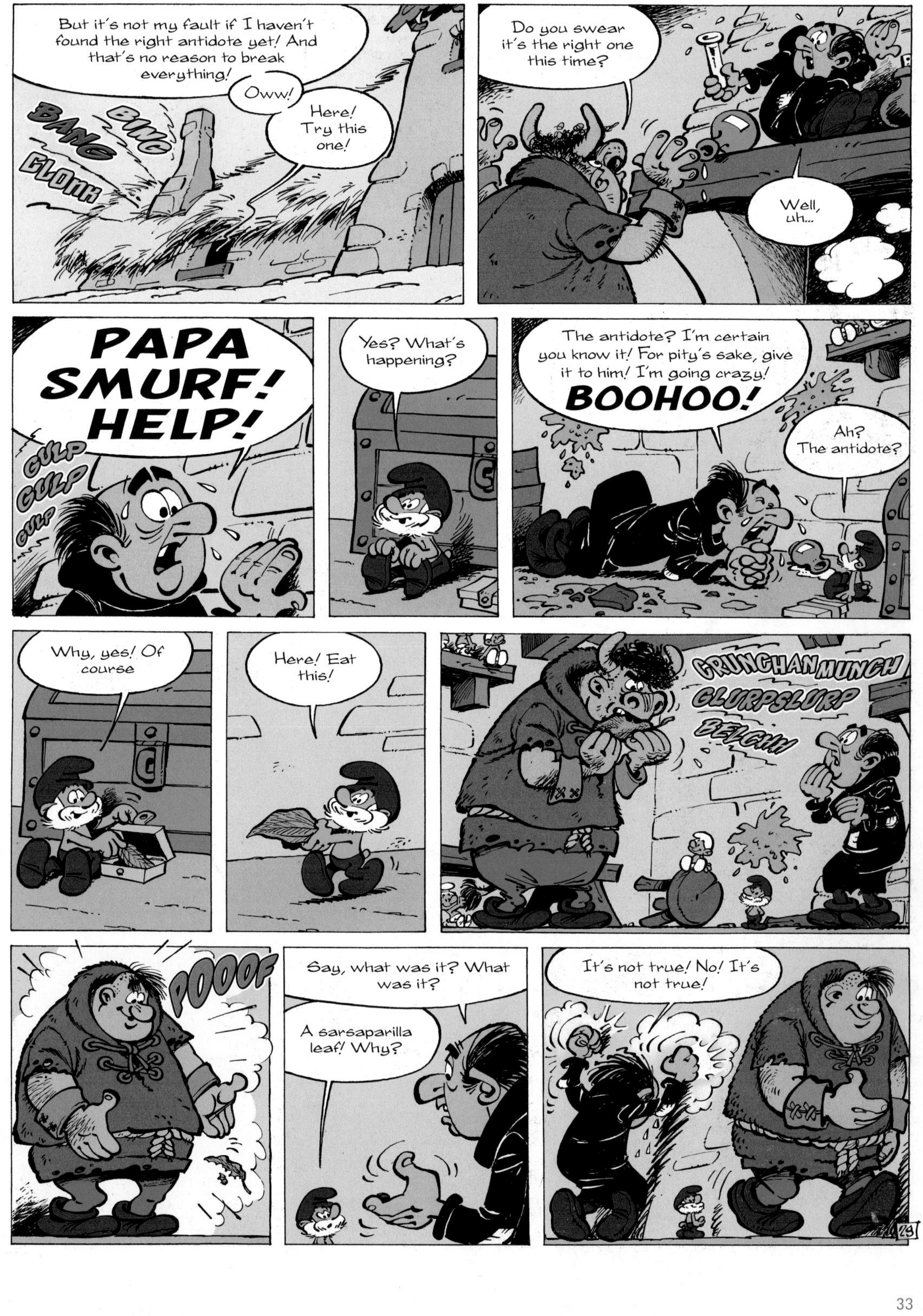

But it's not my fault if I haven't found the right antidote yet! And that's no reason to break everything!
Oww!
BING
BANG
GLONK
Here! Try this one!
Do you swear it's the right one this time?
Well, uh...
PAPA SMURF! HELP!
GULP
GULP
GULP
Yes? What's happening?
The antidote? I'm certain you know it! For pity's sake, give it to him! I'm going crazy! BOOHOO!
Ah? The antidote?
Why, yes! Of course
Here! Eat this!
CRUNCHANMUNCH
GLURPSLURP
BELCHH
POOOF
Say, what was it? What was it?
A sarsaparilla leaf! Why?
It's not true! No! It's not true!
29

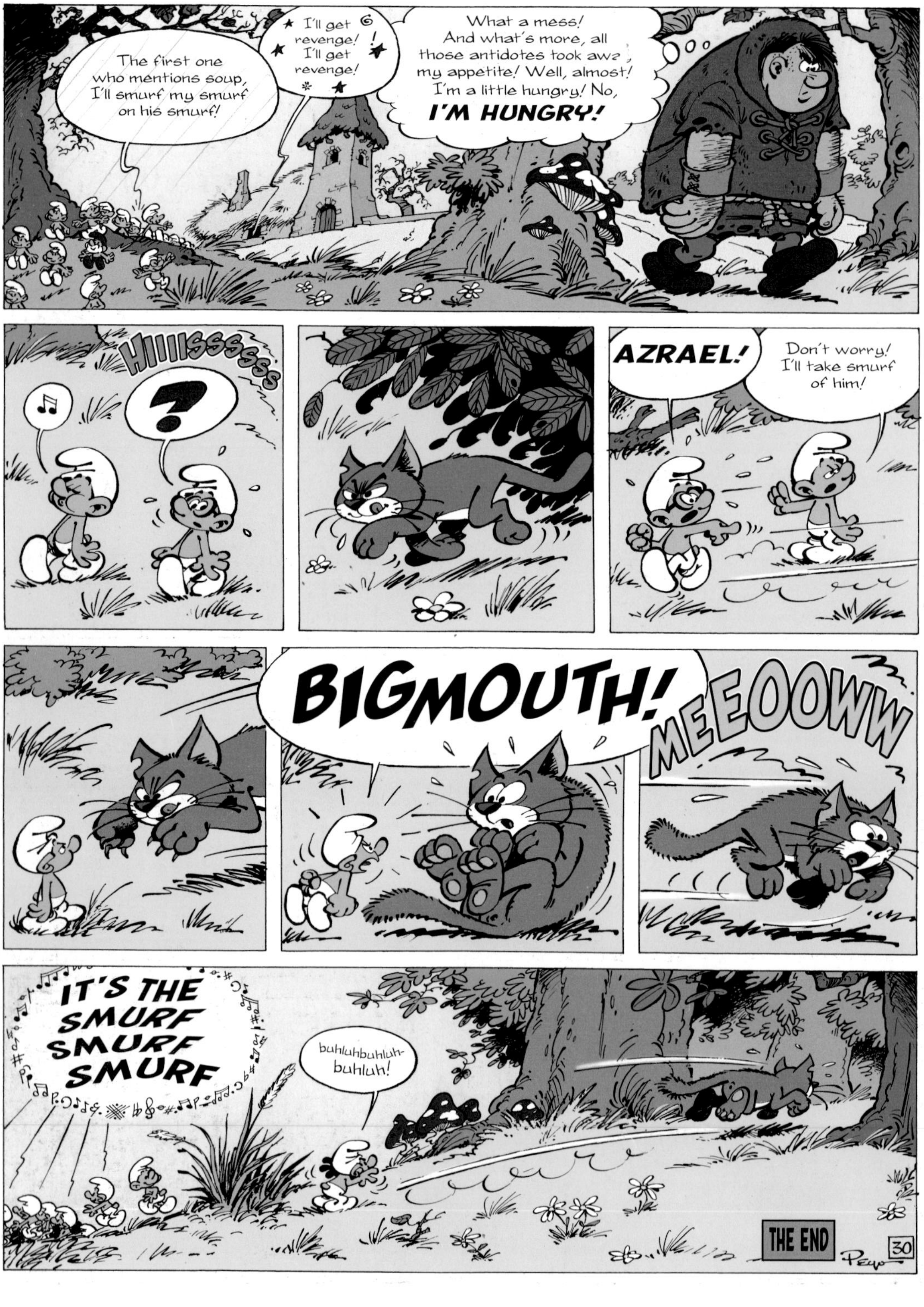
The first one who mentions soup, I'll smurf my smurf on his smurf!
I'll get revenge! I'll get revenge!
What a mess! And what's more, all those antidotes took away my appetite! Well, almost! I'm a little hungry! No, I'M HUNGRY!
HIIIISSSSSSS
AZRAEL!
Don't worry! I'll take smurf of him!
BIGMOUTH!
MEEOOWW
IT'S THE SMURF SMURF SMURF
buhluhbuhluh-buhluh!
THE END
30

GARGAMEL AND THE CROCODILE

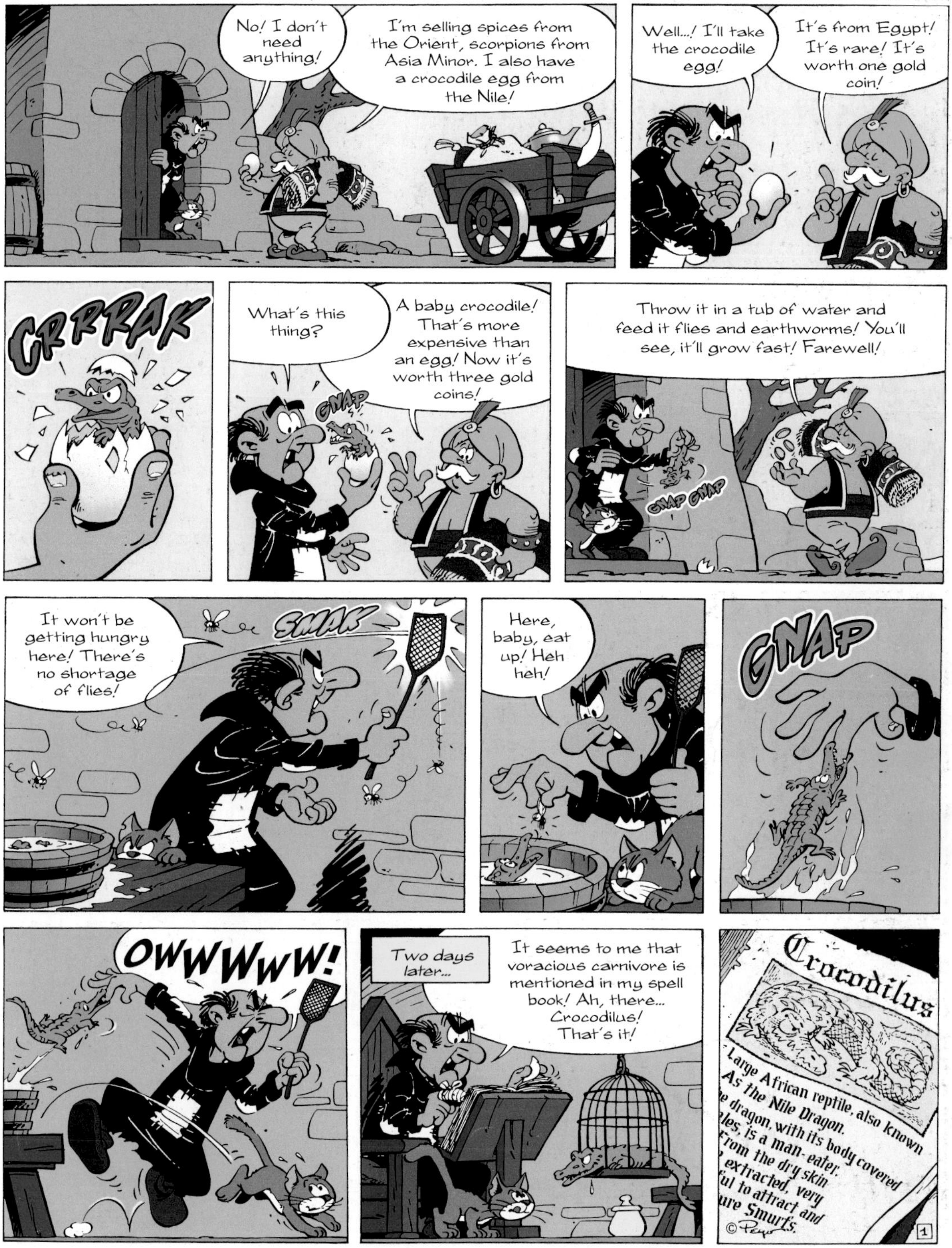
No! I don't need anything!
I'm selling spices from the Orient, scorpions from Asia Minor. I also have a crocodile egg from the Nile!
Well...! I'll take the crocodile egg!
It's from Egypt! It's rare! It's worth one gold coin!
CRRRAK
What's this thing?
A baby crocodile! That's more expensive than an egg! Now it's worth three gold coins!
GNAP
Throw it in a tub of water and feed it flies and earthworms! You'll see, it'll grow fast! Farewell!
GNAP GNAP
It won't be getting hungry here! There's no shortage of flies!
SMAK
Here, baby, eat up! Heh heh!
GNAP
OWWWWW!
Two days later...
It seems to me that voracious carnivore is mentioned in my spell book! Ah, there... Crocodilus! That's it!
Crocodilus
Large African reptile, also known
As the Nile Dragon.
e dragon, with its body covered
les, is a man-eater.
From the dry skin
extracted, very
ful to attract and
ure Smurfs.
© Peyo
1

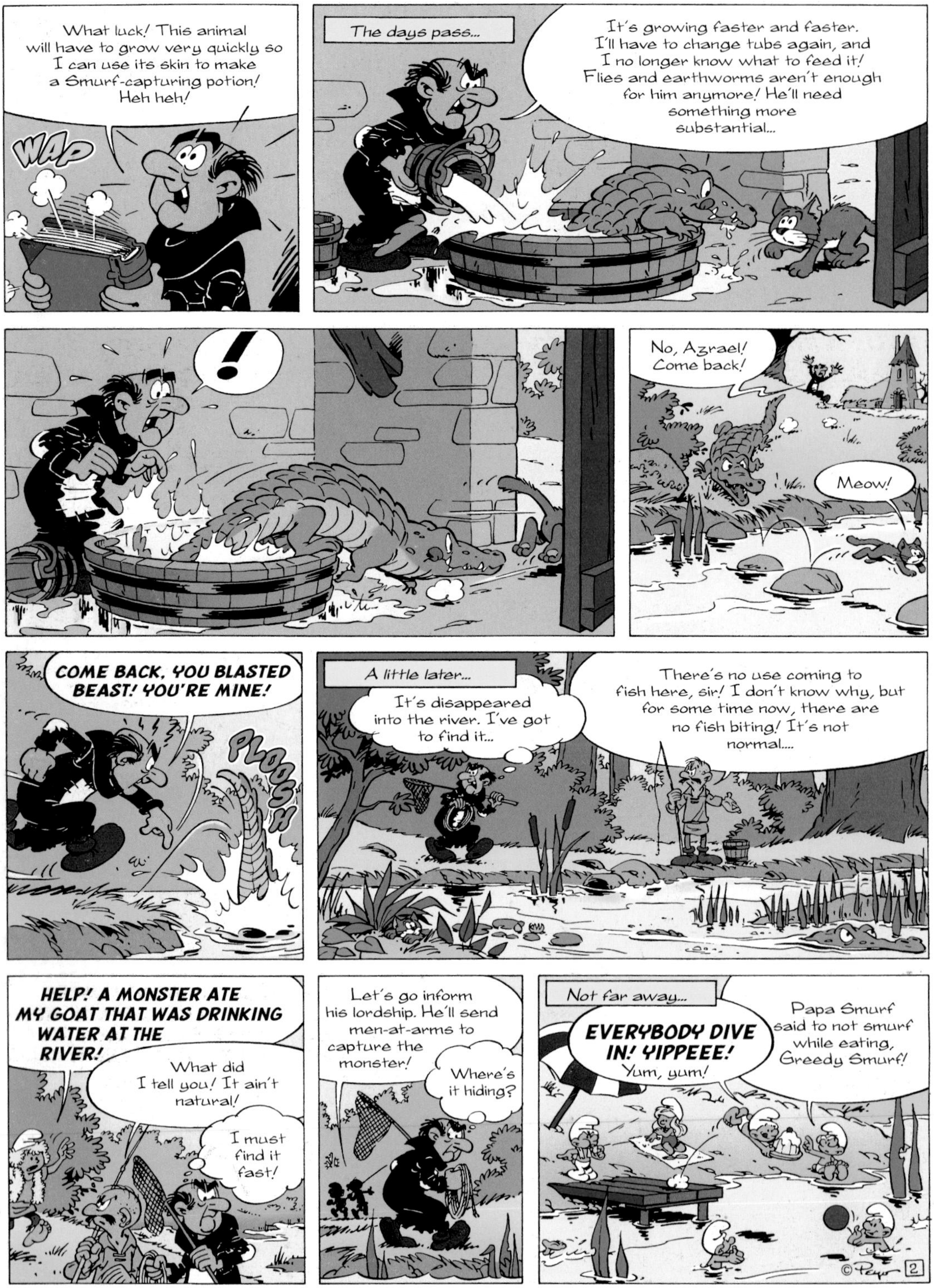
What luck! This animal will have to grow very quickly so I can use its skin to make a Smurf-capturing potion! Heh heh!
WAP
The days pass...
It's growing faster and faster. I'll have to change tubs again, and I no longer know what to feed it! Flies and earthworms aren't enough for him anymore! He'll need something more substantial...
!
No, Azrael! Come back!
Meow!
COME BACK, YOU BLASTED BEAST! YOU'RE MINE!
PLOOSH
A little later...
It's disappeared into the river. I've got to find it...
There's no use coming to fish here, sir! I don't know why, but for some time now, there are no fish biting! It's not normal....
HELP! A MONSTER ATE MY GOAT THAT WAS DRINKING WATER AT THE RIVER!
What did I tell you! It ain't natural!
I must find it fast!
Let's go inform his lordship. He'll send men-at-arms to capture the monster!
Where's it hiding?
Not far away...
EVERYBODY DIVE IN! YIPPEEE!
Yum, yum!
Papa Smurf said to not smurf while eating, Greedy Smurf!
© Peyo 2

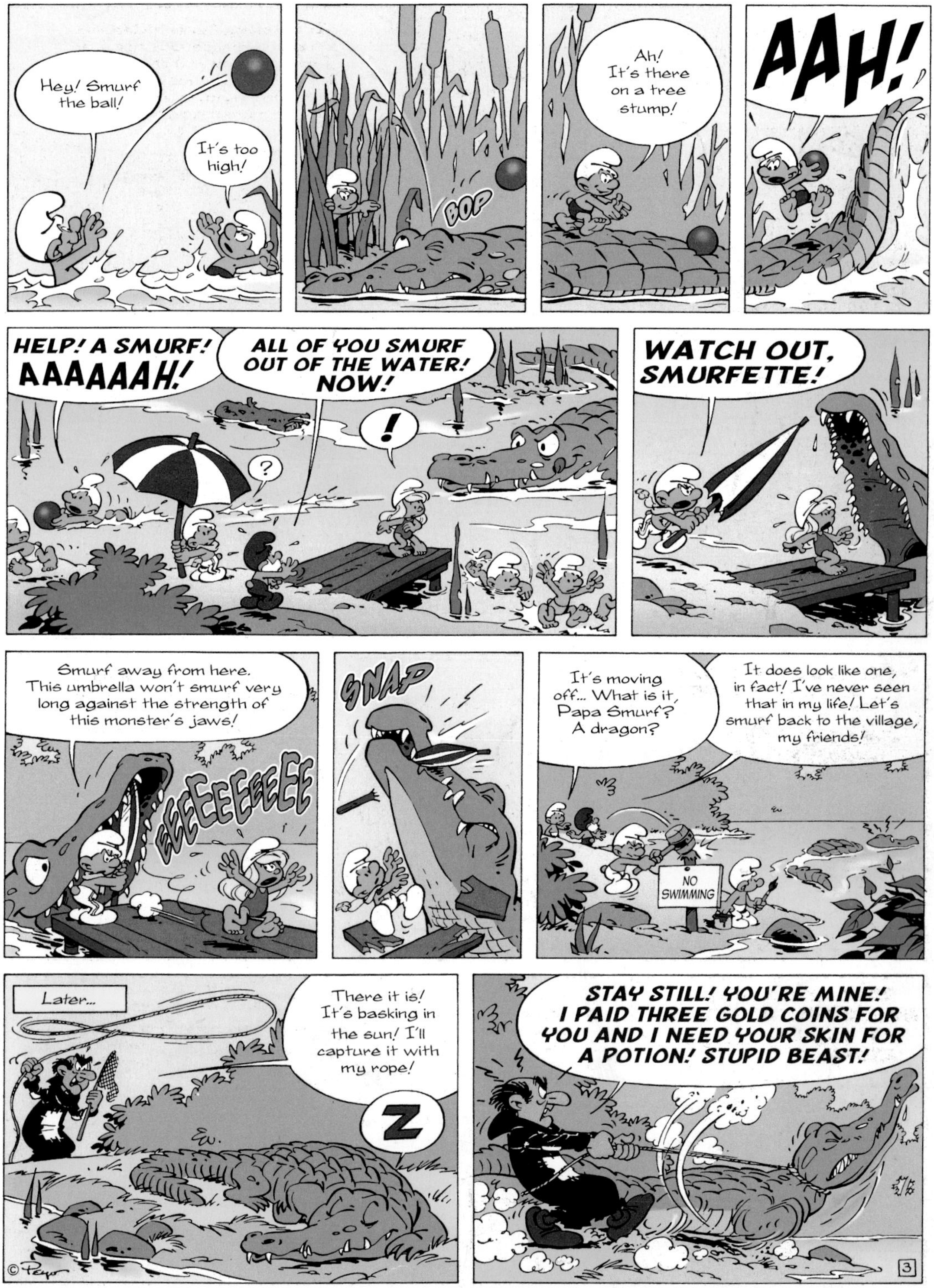
Hey! Smurf the ball!
It's too high!
BOP
Ah! It's there on a tree stump!
AAH!
HELP! A SMURF! AAAAAAH!
ALL OF YOU SMURF OUT OF THE WATER! NOW!
?
!
WATCH OUT, SMURFETTE!
Smurf away from here. This umbrella won't smurf very long against the strength of this monster's jaws!
EEEEEEEEEE
SNAP
It's moving off... What is it, Papa Smurf? A dragon?
It does look like one, in fact! I've never seen that in my life! Let's smurf back to the village, my friends!
NO SWIMMING
Later...
There it is! It's basking in the sun! I'll capture it with my rope!
Z
STAY STILL! YOU'RE MINE! I PAID THREE GOLD COINS FOR YOU AND I NEED YOUR SKIN FOR A POTION! STUPID BEAST!
© Peyo
3

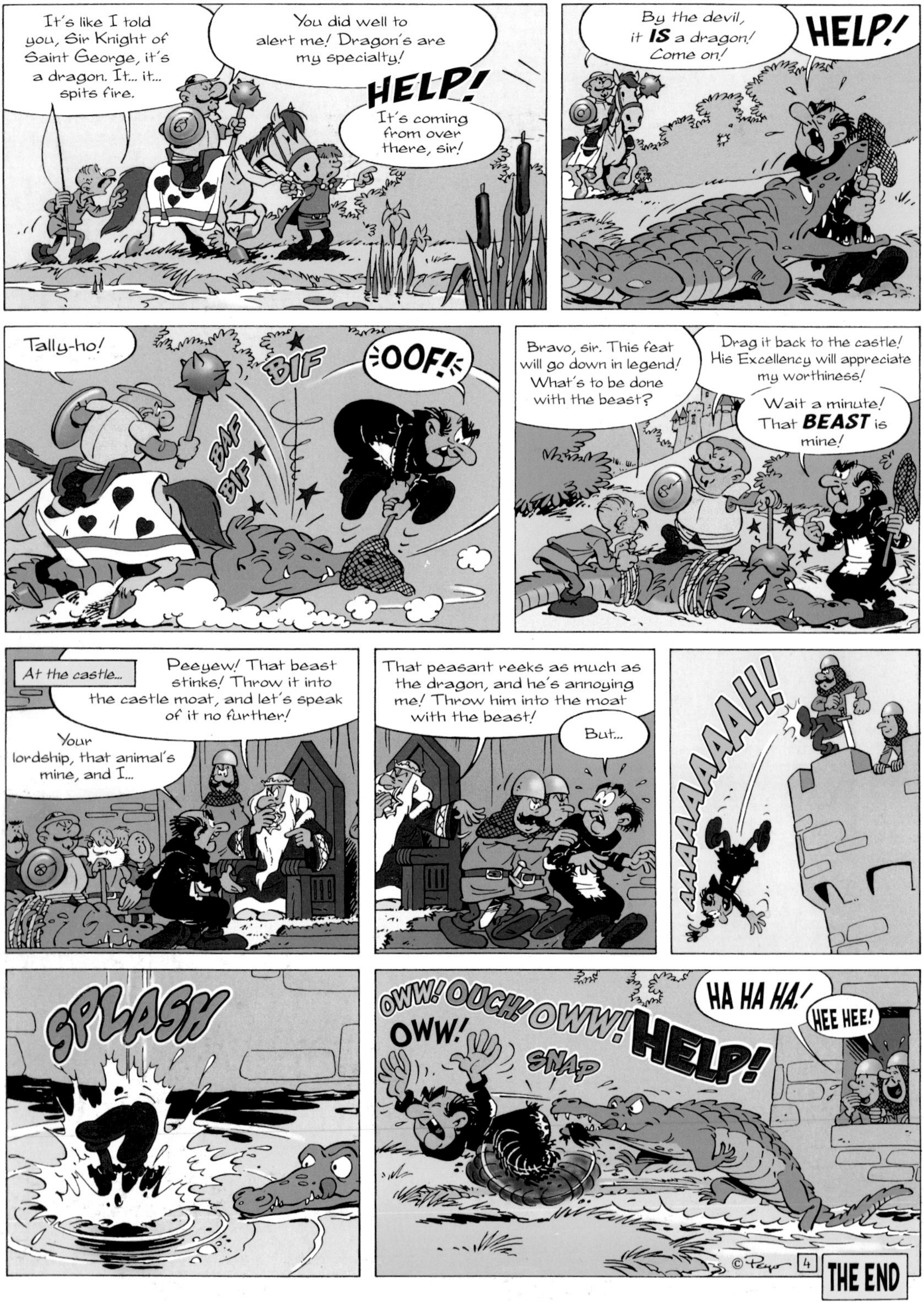

It's like I told you, Sir Knight of Saint George, it's a dragon. It... it... spits fire.
You did well to alert me! Dragon's are my specialty!
HELP!
It's coming from over there, sir!
By the devil, it IS a dragon! Come on!
HELP!
Tally-ho!
BIF
OOF!
BAF
BIF
Bravo, sir. This feat will go down in legend! What's to be done with the beast?
Drag it back to the castle! His Excellency will appreciate my worthiness!
Wait a minute! That BEAST is mine!
At the castle...
Peeyew! That beast stinks! Throw it into the castle moat, and let's speak of it no further!
Your lordship, that animal's mine, and I...
That peasant reeks as much as the dragon, and he's annoying me! Throw him into the moat with the beast!
But...
AAAAAAAAH!
SPLASH
OWW! OUCH! OWW!
OWW!
SNAP
HELP!
HA HA HA!
HEE HEE!
© Peyo
4
THE END

THE CLOCKWORK SMURF

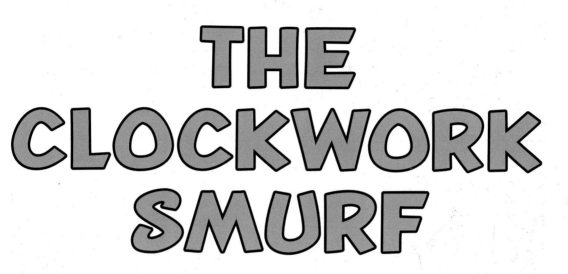

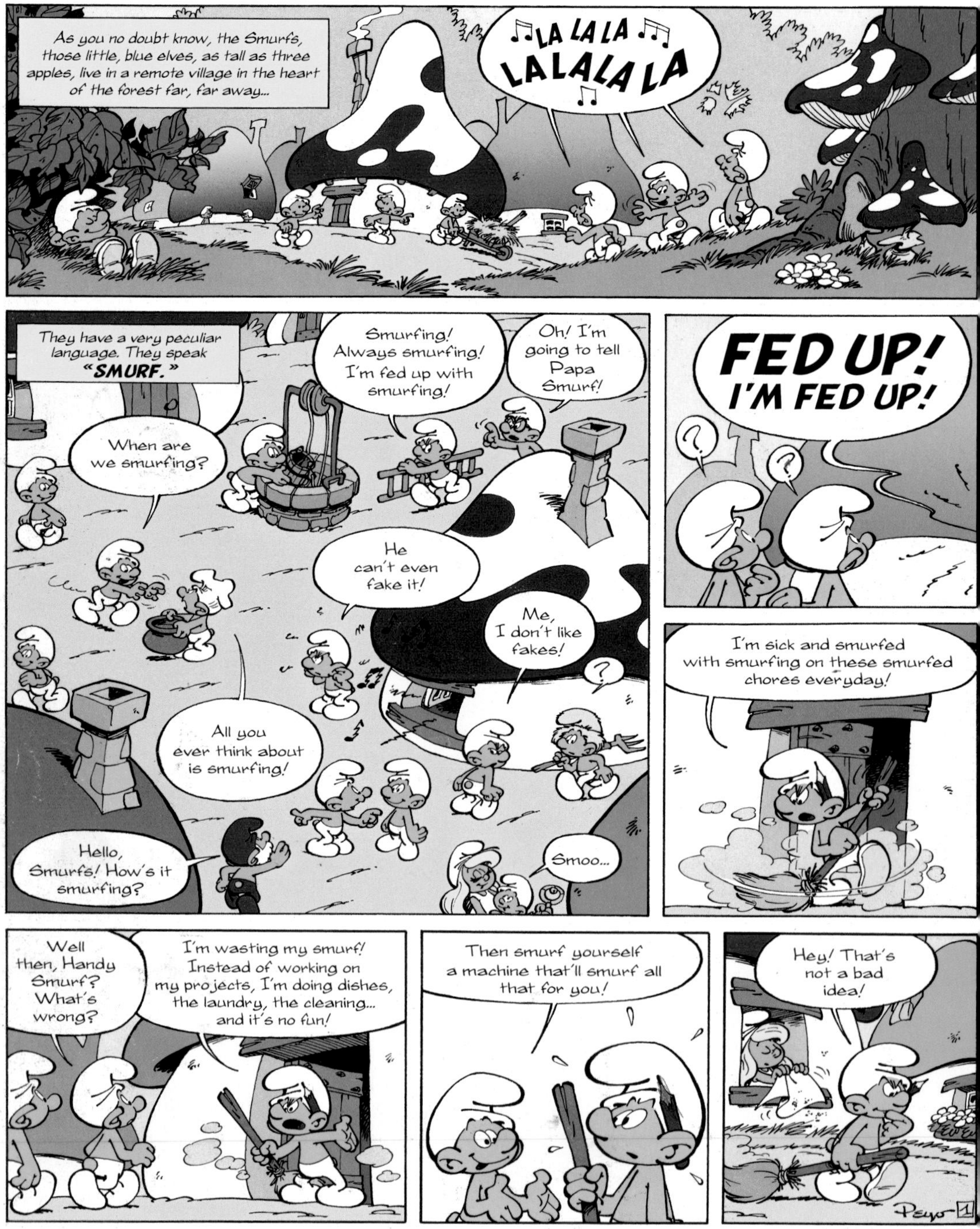

As you no doubt know, the Smurfs, those little, blue elves, as tall as three apples, live in a remote village in the heart of the forest far, far away...
LA LA LA LALALALA
They have a very peculiar language. They speak "SMURF."
Smurfing! Always smurfing! I'm fed up with smurfing!
Oh! I'm going to tell Papa Smurf!
When are we smurfing?
He can't even fake it!
Me, I don't like fakes!
?
All you ever think about is smurfing!
Hello, Smurfs! How's it smurfing?
Smoo...
FED UP! I'M FED UP!
?
?
I'm sick and smurfed with smurfing on these smurfed chores everyday!
Well then, Handy Smurf? What's wrong?
I'm wasting my smurf! Instead of working on my projects, I'm doing dishes, the laundry, the cleaning... and it's no fun!
Then smurf yourself a machine that'll smurf all that for you!
Hey! That's not a bad idea!
Peyo
1

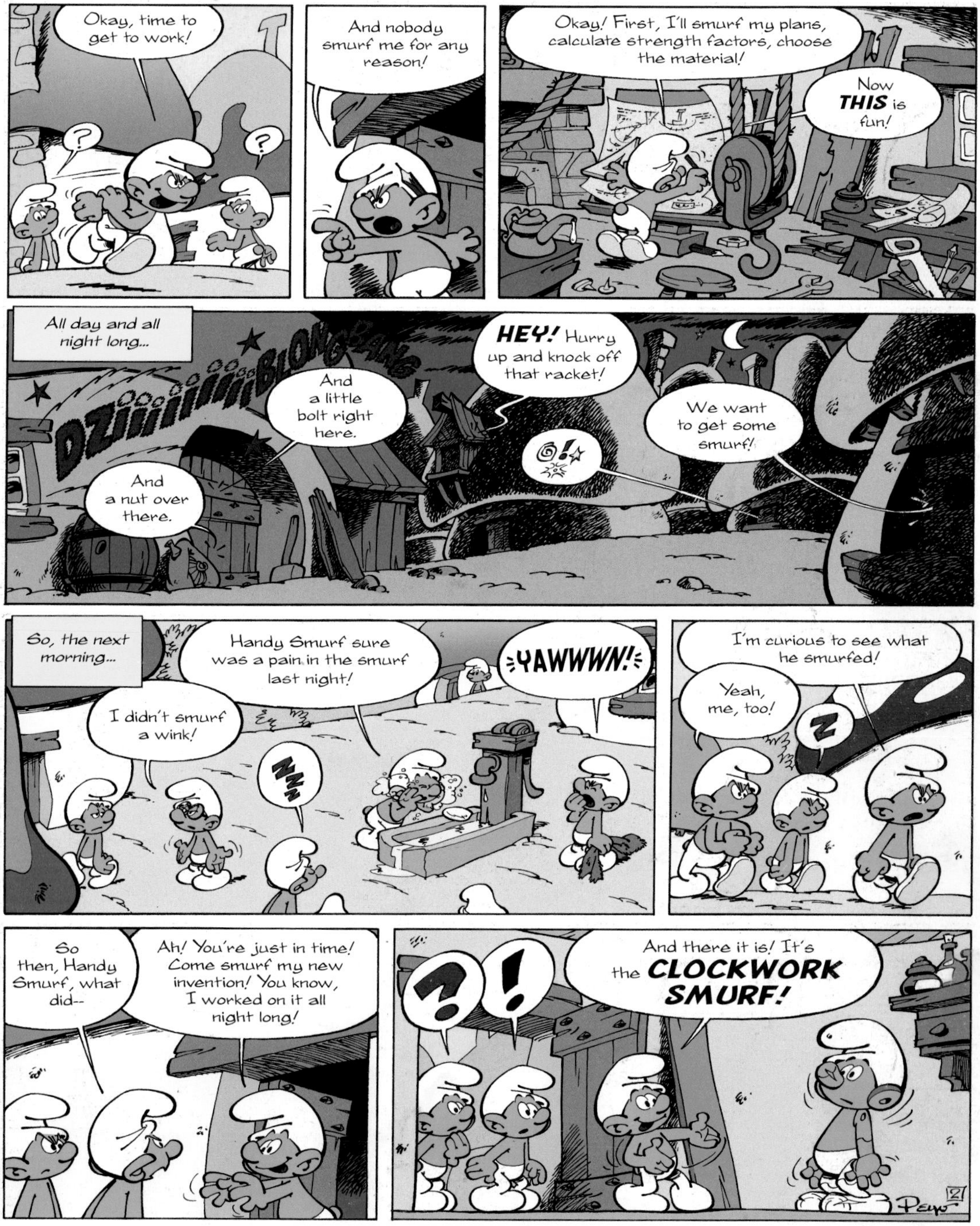
Okay, time to get to work!
?
?
And nobody smurf me for any reason!
Okay! First, I'll smurf my plans, calculate strength factors, choose the material!
Now THIS is fun!
All day and all night long...
DZiiiiiiiiiiiBLONGBANG
And a nut over there.
And a little bolt right here.
HEY! Hurry up and knock off that racket!
We want to get some smurf!
So, the next morning...
I didn't smurf a wink!
Handy Smurf sure was a pain in the smurf last night!
YAWWWN!
I'm curious to see what he smurfed!
Yeah, me, too!
So then, Handy Smurf, what did--
Ah! You're just in time! Come smurf my new invention! You know, I worked on it all night long!
?
!
And there it is! It's the CLOCKWORK SMURF!
Peyo

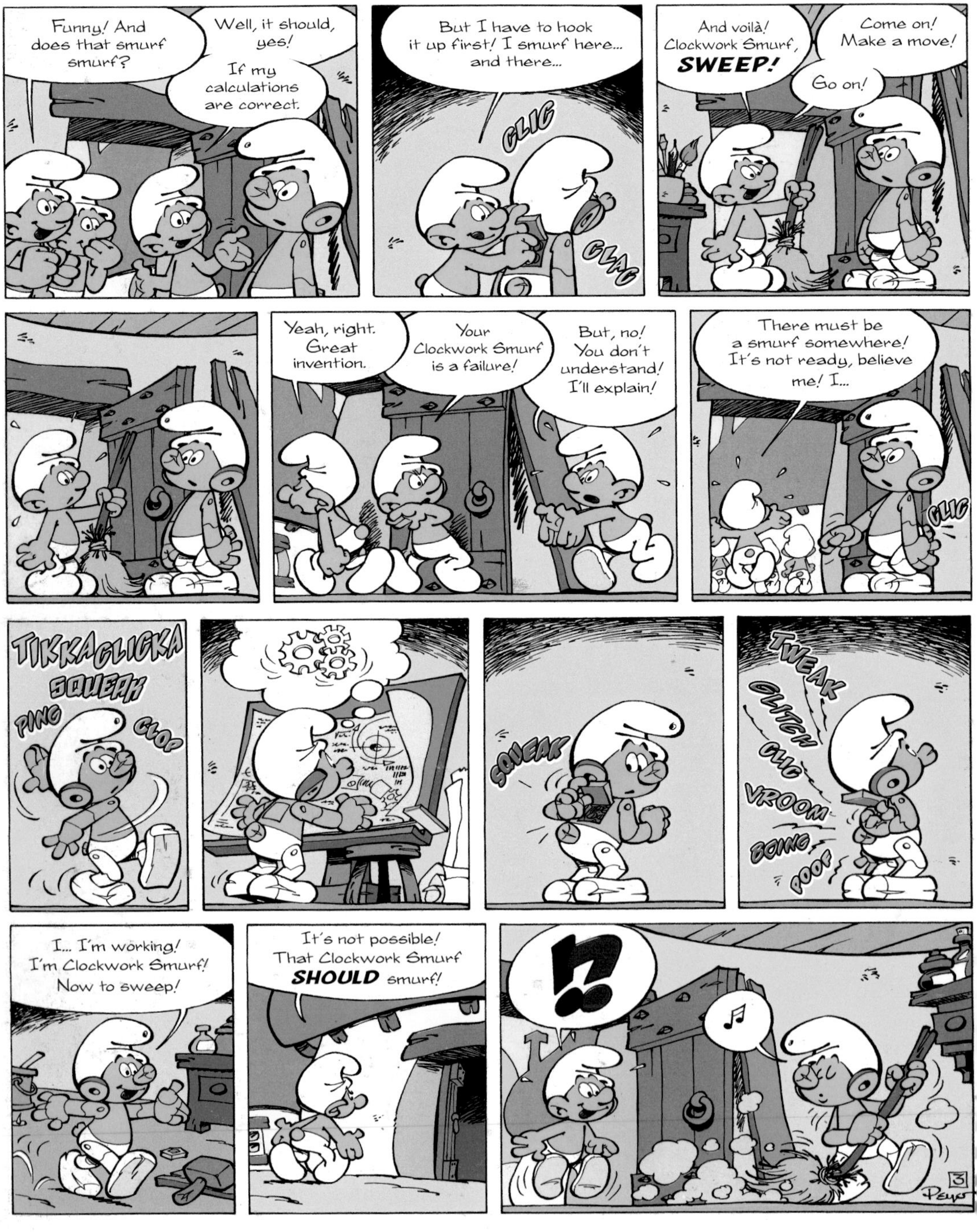
Funny! And does that smurf smurf?
Well, it should, yes!
If my calculations are correct.
But I have to hook it up first! I smurf here... and there...
CLIC
CLAC
And voilà! Clockwork Smurf, **SWEEP!**
Come on! Make a move!
Go on!
Yeah, right. Great invention.
Your Clockwork Smurf is a failure!
But, no! You don't understand! I'll explain!
There must be a smurf somewhere! It's not ready, believe me! I...
CLIC
TIKKACLICKA
SQUEAK
PING
CLOP
SQUEAK
TWEAK
GLITCH
CLIC
VROOM
BOING
POOF
I... I'm working! I'm Clockwork Smurf! Now to sweep!
It's not possible! That Clockwork Smurf **SHOULD** smurf!
3

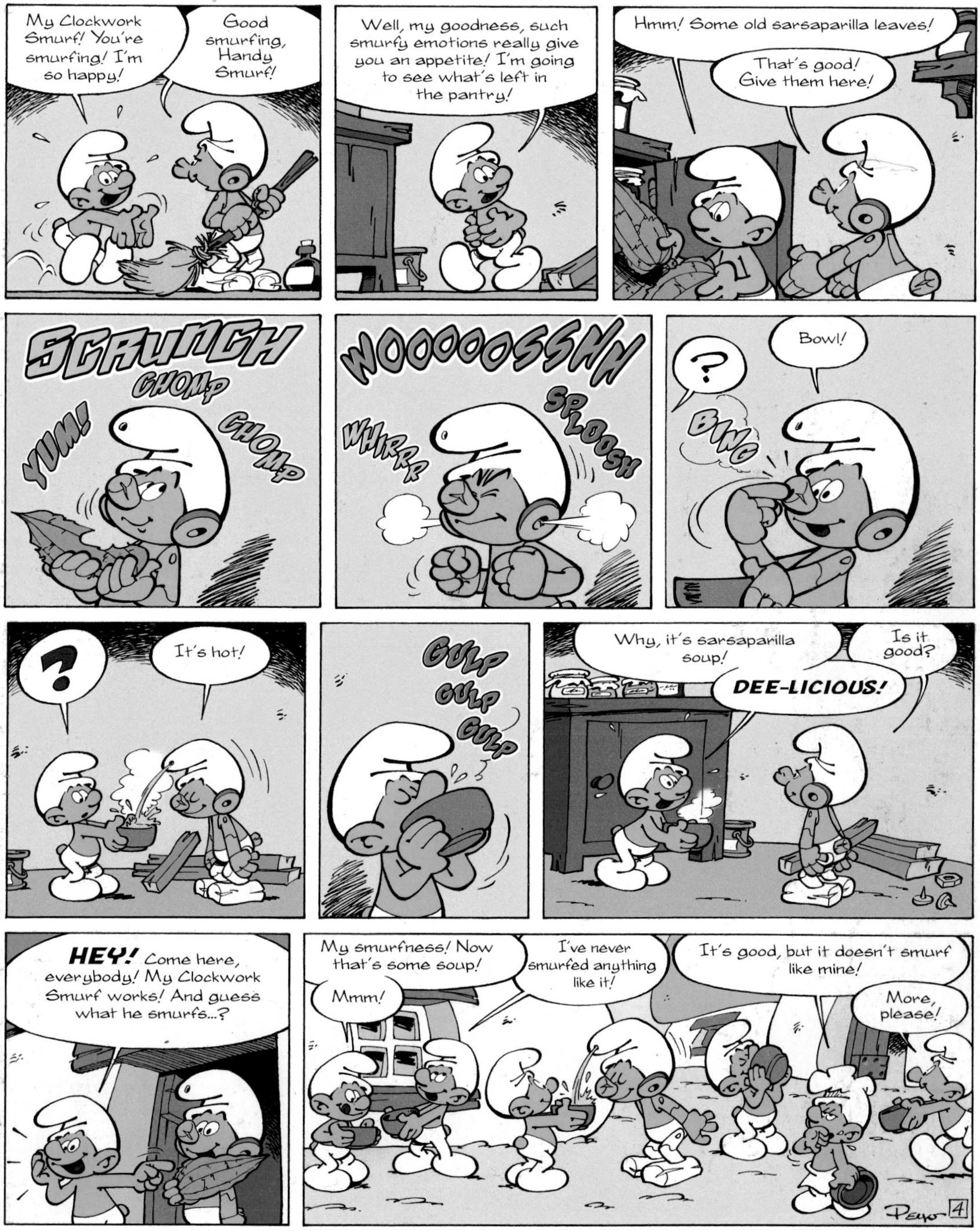

My Clockwork Smurf! You're smurfing! I'm so happy!
Good smurfing, Handy Smurf!
Well, my goodness, such smurfy emotions really give you an appetite! I'm going to see what's left in the pantry!
Hmm! Some old sarsaparilla leaves!
That's good! Give them here!
SCRUNCH
CHOMP
CHOMP
YUM!
WOOOOOOSSHH
WHIRRR
SPLOOSH
?
Bowl!
BING
?
It's hot!
GULP
GULP
GULP
Why, it's sarsaparilla soup!
Is it good?
DEE-LICIOUS!
HEY! Come here, everybody! My Clockwork Smurf works! And guess what he smurfs...?
My smurfness! Now that's some soup!
Mmm!
I've never smurfed anything like it!
It's good, but it doesn't smurf like mine!
More, please!
Peyo
4

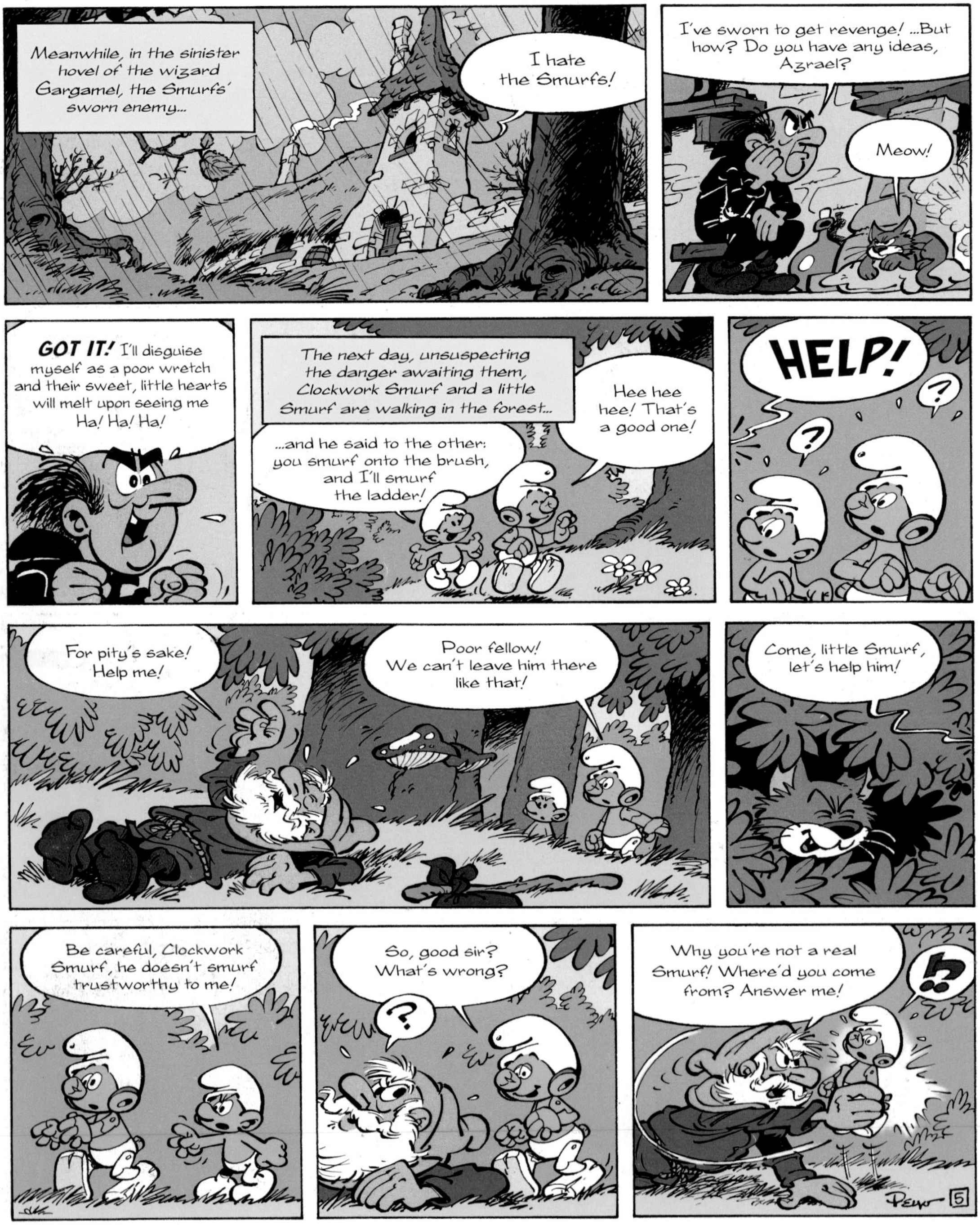
Meanwhile, in the sinister hovel of the wizard Gargamel, the Smurfs' sworn enemy...
I hate the Smurfs!
I've sworn to get revenge! ...But how? Do you have any ideas, Azrael?
Meow!
GOT IT! I'll disguise myself as a poor wretch and their sweet, little hearts will melt upon seeing me Ha! Ha! Ha!
The next day, unsuspecting the danger awaiting them, Clockwork Smurf and a little Smurf are walking in the forest...
...and he said to the other: you smurf onto the brush, and I'll smurf the ladder!
Hee hee hee! That's a good one!
HELP!
?
?
For pity's sake! Help me!
Poor fellow! We can't leave him there like that!
Come, little Smurf, let's help him!
Be careful, Clockwork Smurf, he doesn't smurf trustworthy to me!
So, good sir? What's wrong?
?
Why you're not a real Smurf! Where'd you come from? Answer me!
Peyo
5

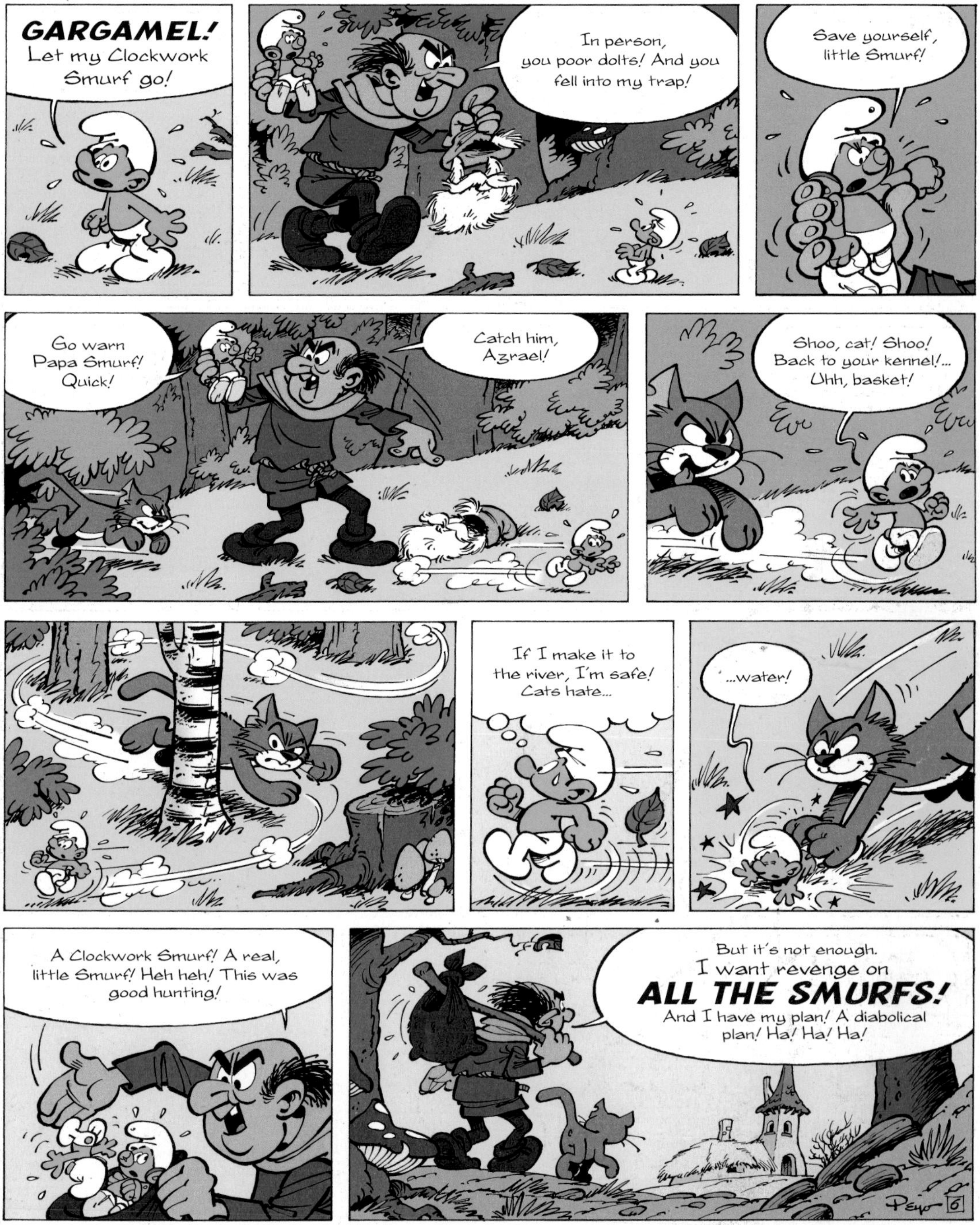
GARGAMEL! Let my Clockwork Smurf go!
In person, you poor dolts! And you fell into my trap!
Save yourself, little Smurf!
Go warn Papa Smurf! Quick!
Catch him, Azrael!
Shoo, cat! Shoo! Back to your kennel!... Uhh, basket!
If I make it to the river, I'm safe! Cats hate...
...water!
A Clockwork Smurf! A real, little Smurf! Heh heh! This was good hunting!
But it's not enough. I want revenge on ALL THE SMURFS! And I have my plan! A diabolical plan! Ha! Ha! Ha!
Peyo
6

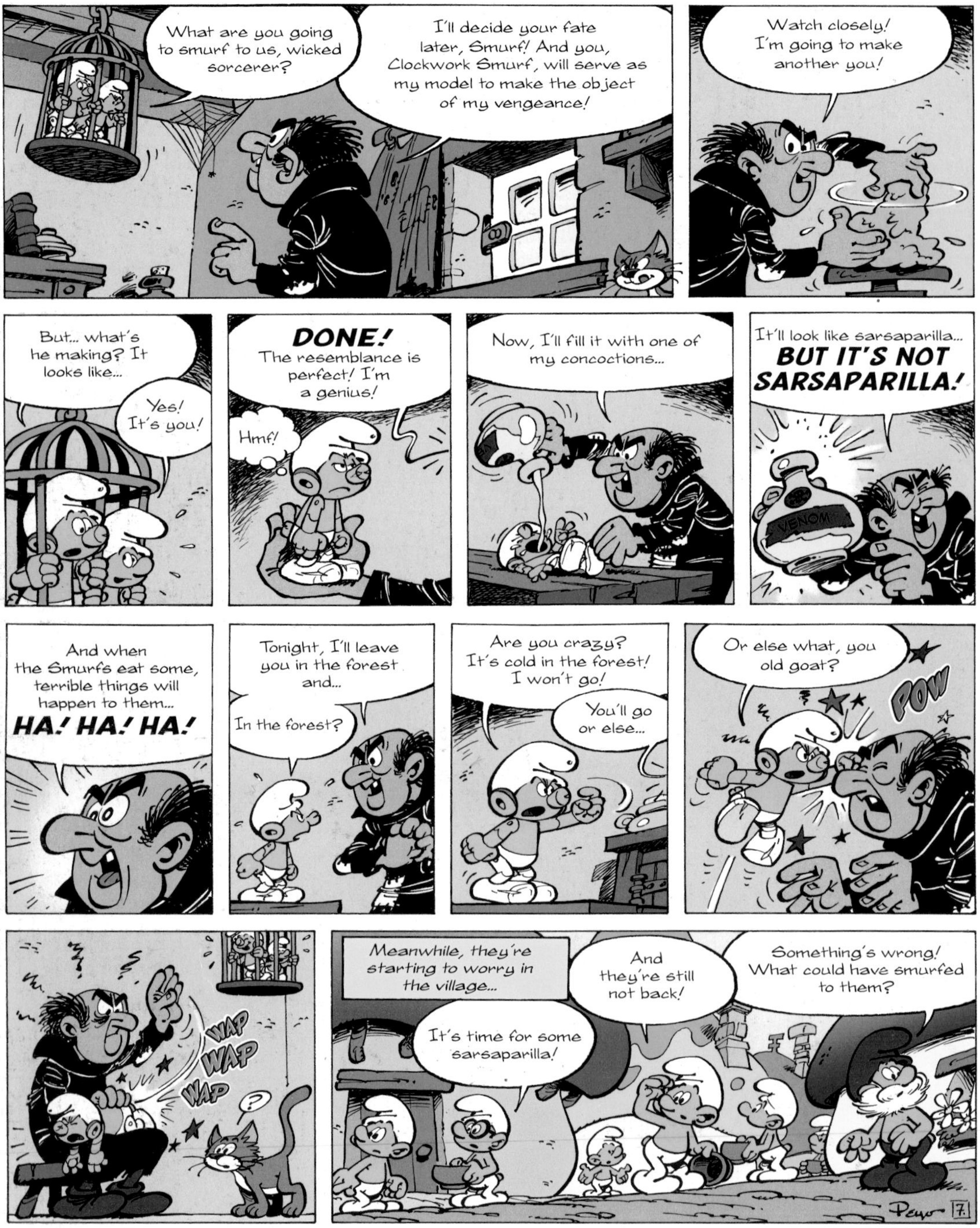
What are you going to smurf to us, wicked sorcerer?
I'll decide your fate later, Smurf! And you, Clockwork Smurf, will serve as my model to make the object of my vengeance!
Watch closely! I'm going to make another you!
But... what's he making? It looks like...
Yes! It's you!
DONE! The resemblance is perfect! I'm a genius!
Hmf!
Now, I'll fill it with one of my concoctions...
It'll look like sarsaparilla... BUT IT'S NOT SARSAPARILLA!
VENOM
And when the Smurfs eat some, terrible things will happen to them... HA! HA! HA!
Tonight, I'll leave you in the forest and...
In the forest?
Are you crazy? It's cold in the forest! I won't go!
You'll go or else...
Or else what, you old goat?
POW
WAP
WAP
WAP
?
Meanwhile, they're starting to worry in the village...
It's time for some sarsaparilla!
And they're still not back!
Something's wrong! What could have smurfed to them?
Peyo
7

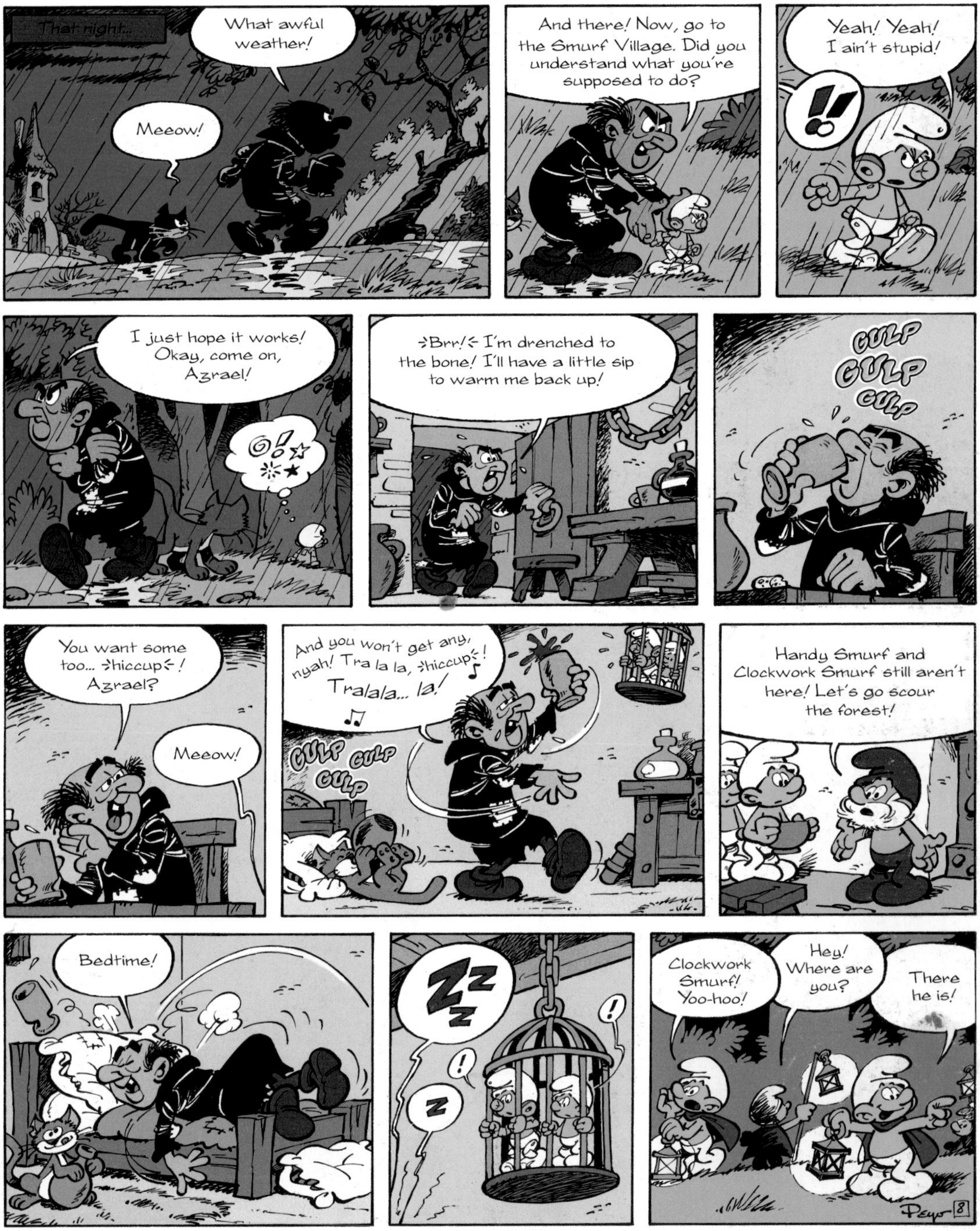
That night...
What awful weather!
Meeow!
And there! Now, go to the Smurf Village. Did you understand what you're supposed to do?
Yeah! Yeah! I ain't stupid!
I just hope it works! Okay, come on, Azrael!
>Brr!< I'm drenched to the bone! I'll have a little sip to warm me back up!
GULP GULP GULP
You want some too... >hiccup< ! Azrael?
Meeow!
And you won't get any, nyah! Tra la la, >hiccup< ! Tralala... la!
GULP GULP GULP
Handy Smurf and Clockwork Smurf still aren't here! Let's go scour the forest!
Bedtime!
Z Z Z
Z
Clockwork Smurf! Yoo-hoo!
Hey! Where are you?
There he is!
Peyo 8

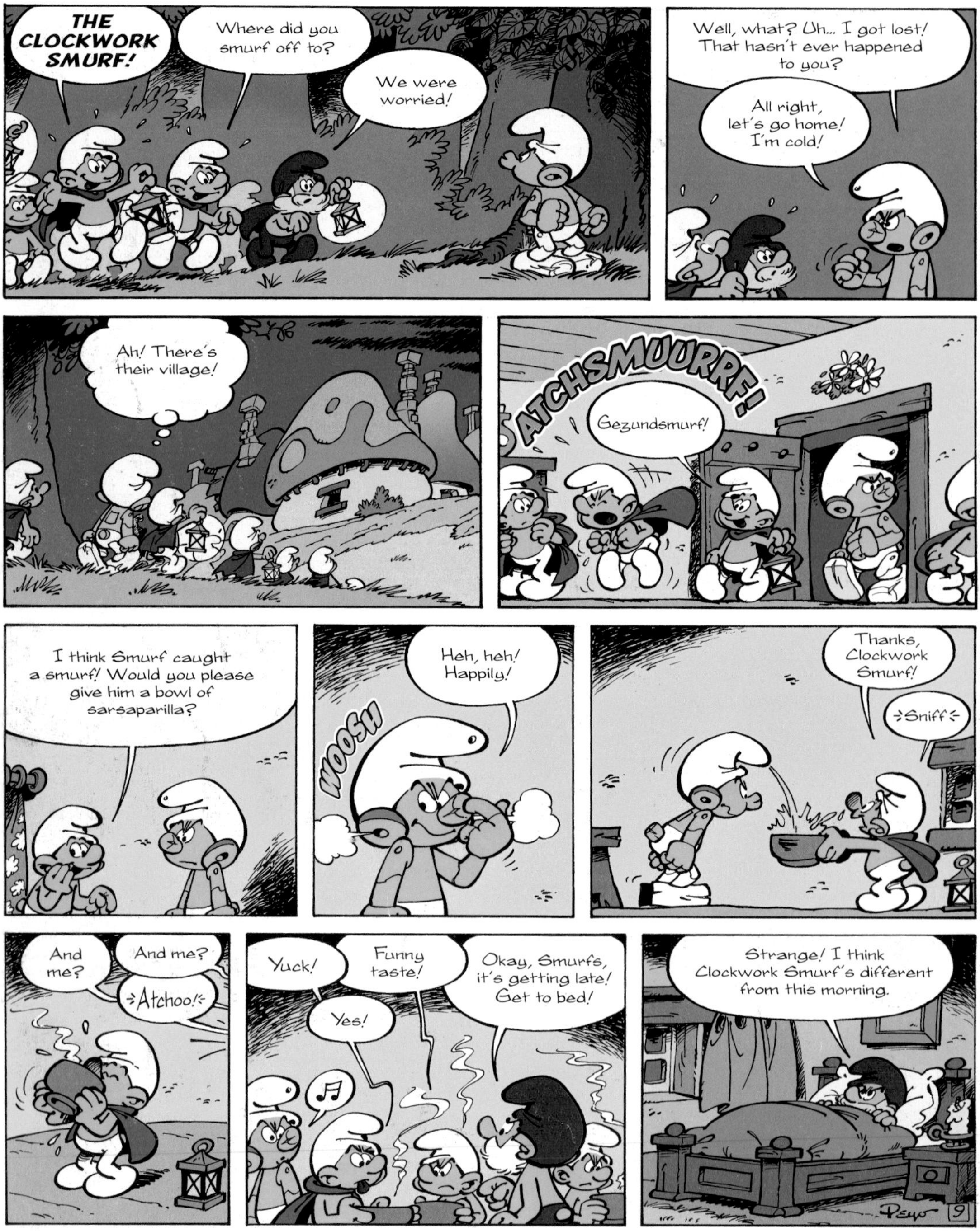
THE CLOCKWORK SMURF!
Where did you smurf off to?
We were worried!
Well, what? Uh... I got lost! That hasn't ever happened to you?
All right, let's go home! I'm cold!
Ah! There's their village!
ATCHSMUURRF!
Gezundsmurf!
I think Smurf caught a smurf! Would you please give him a bowl of sarsaparilla?
WOOSH
Heh, heh! Happily!
Thanks, Clockwork Smurf!
Sniff
And me?
And me?
Atchoo!
Yuck!
Funny taste!
Yes!
Okay, Smurfs, it's getting late! Get to bed!
Strange! I think Clockwork Smurf's different from this morning.
Peyo
9

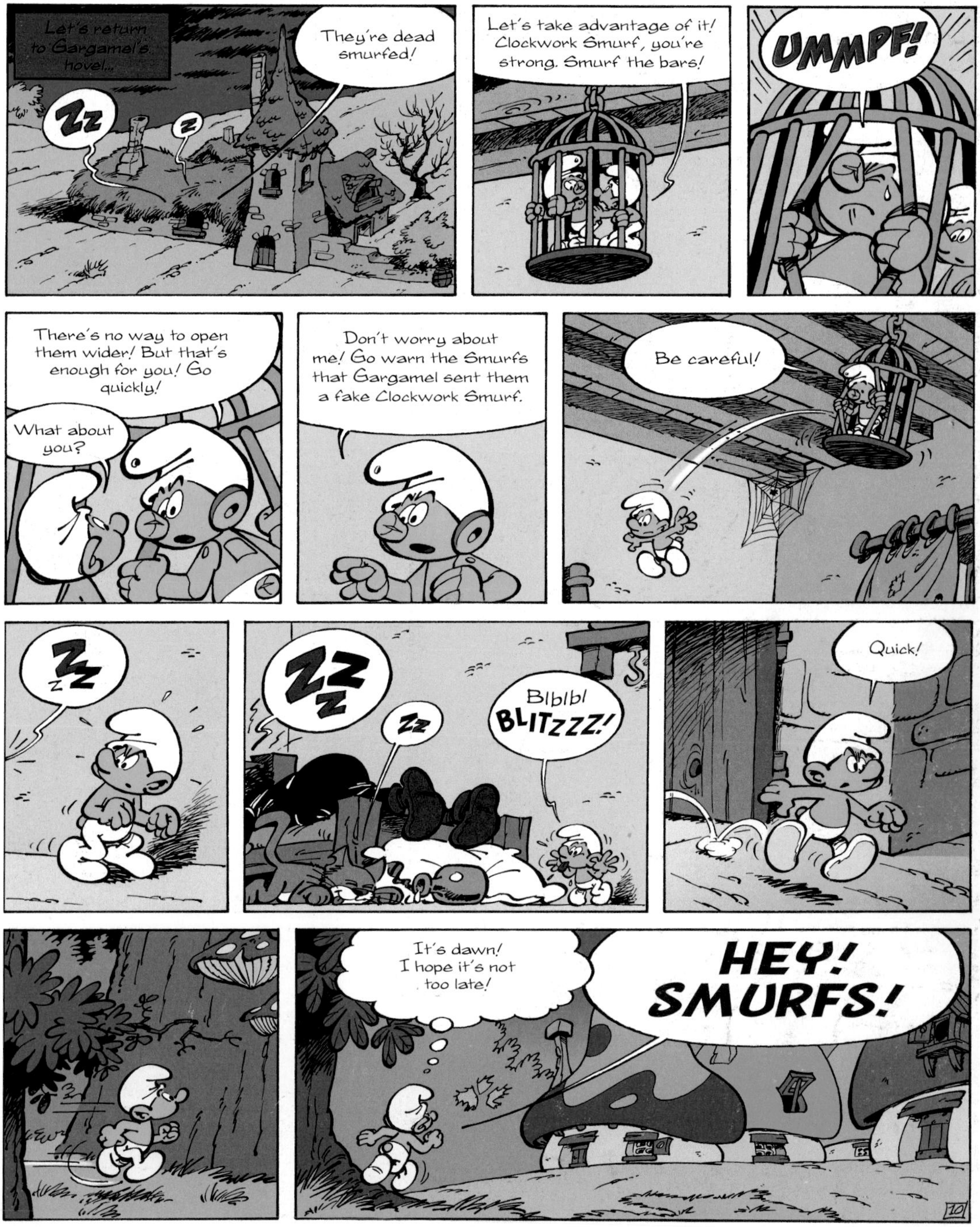
Let's return to Gargamel's hovel...
ZZ
Z
They're dead smurfed!
Let's take advantage of it! Clockwork Smurf, you're strong. Smurf the bars!
UMMPF!
There's no way to open them wider! But that's enough for you! Go quickly!
What about you?
Don't worry about me! Go warn the Smurfs that Gargamel sent them a fake Clockwork Smurf.
Be careful!
ZZZ
ZZZ
ZZ
Blblbl BLITZZZ!
Quick!
It's dawn! I hope it's not too late!
HEY! SMURFS!
10

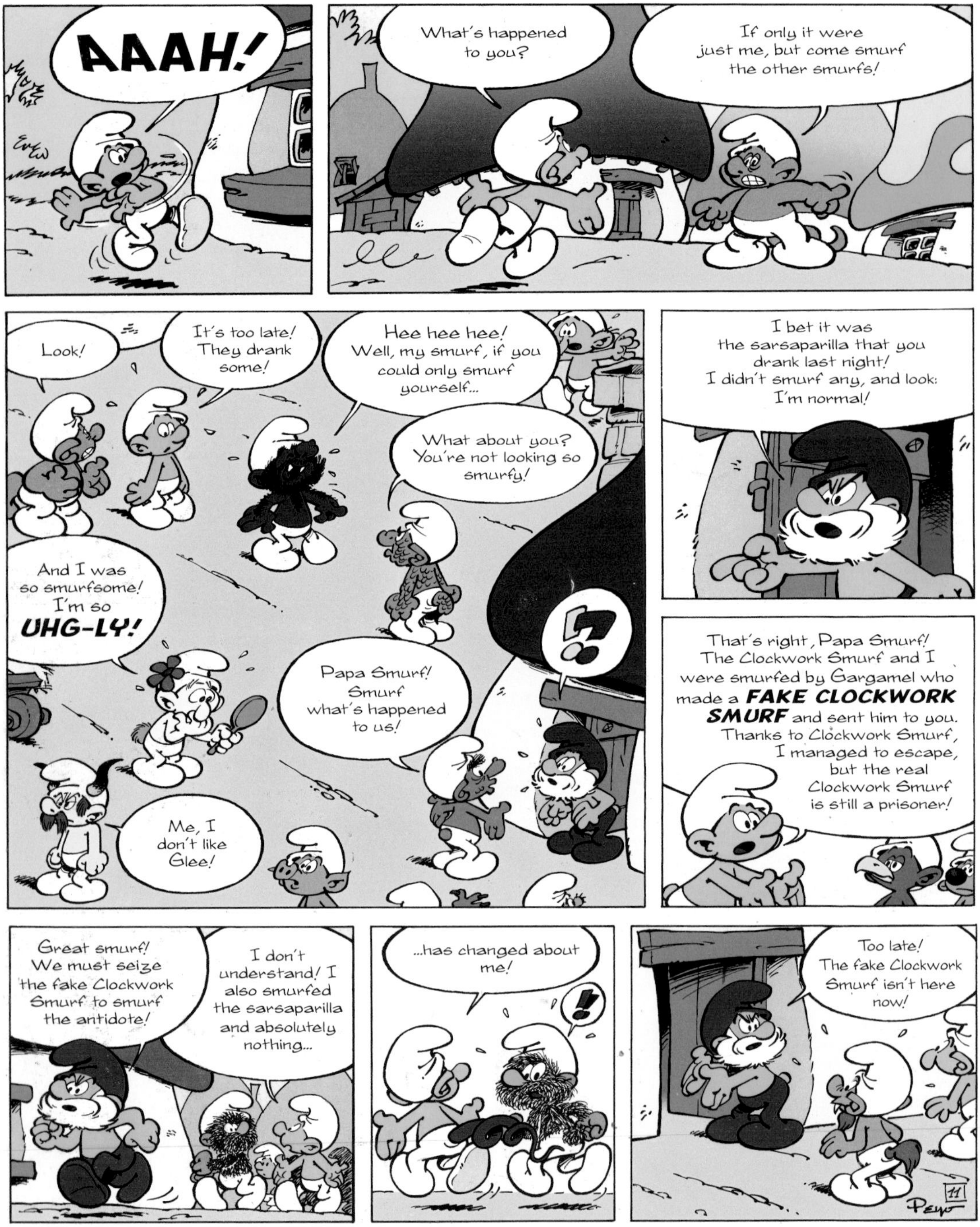
AAAH!
What's happened to you?
If only it were just me, but come smurf the other smurfs!
Look!
It's too late! They drank some!
Hee hee hee! Well, my smurf, if you could only smurf yourself...
What about you? You're not looking so smurfy!
I bet it was the sarsaparilla that you drank last night! I didn't smurf any, and look: I'm normal!
And I was so smurfsome! I'm so UHG-LY!
Papa Smurf! Smurf what's happened to us!
?
Me, I don't like Glee!
That's right, Papa Smurf! The Clockwork Smurf and I were smurfed by Gargamel who made a FAKE CLOCKWORK SMURF and sent him to you. Thanks to Clockwork Smurf, I managed to escape, but the real Clockwork Smurf is still a prisoner!
Great smurf! We must seize the fake Clockwork Smurf to smurf the antidote!
I don't understand! I also smurfed the sarsaparilla and absolutely nothing...
...has changed about me!
!
Too late! The fake Clockwork Smurf isn't here now!
11
Peyo

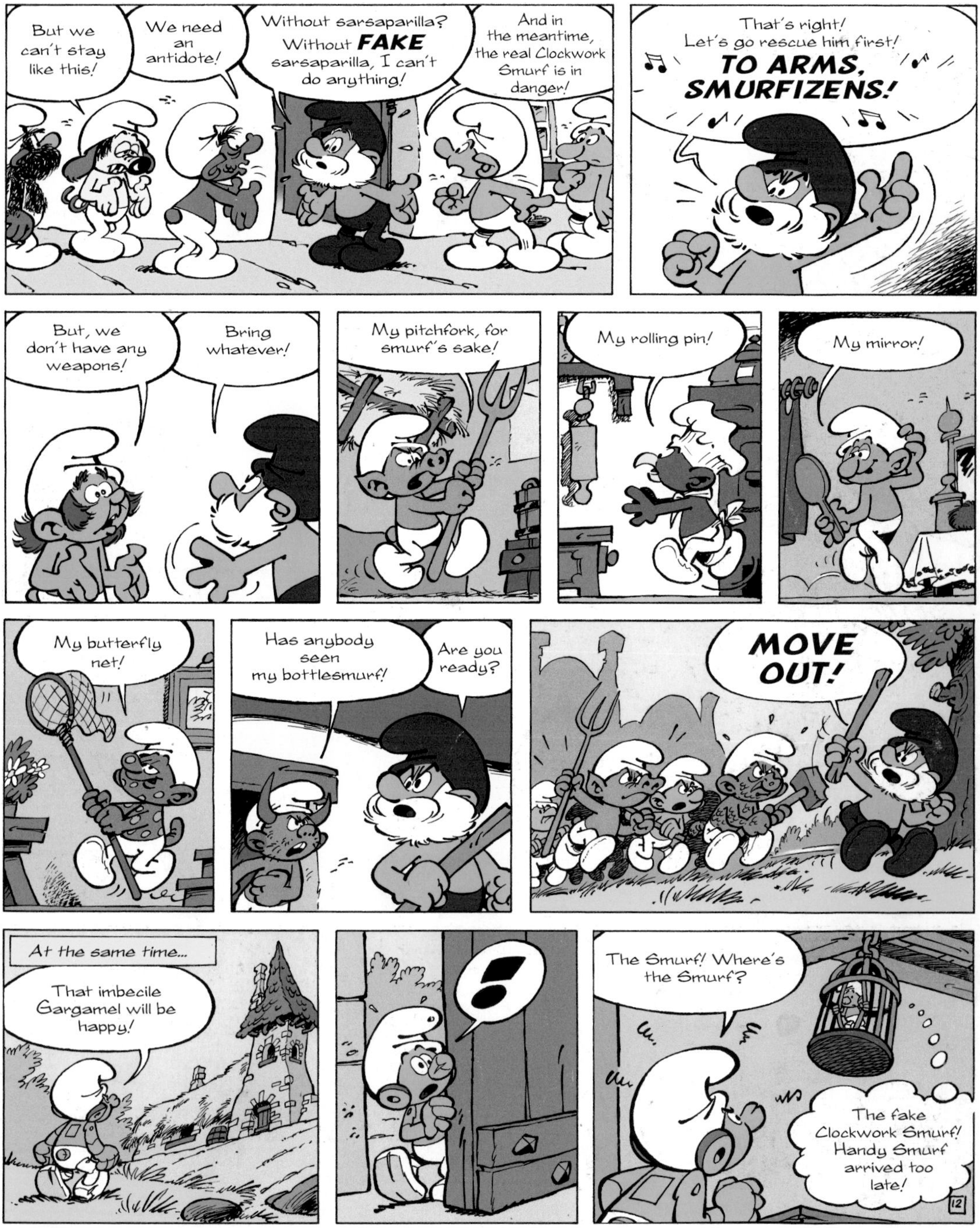

But we can't stay like this!
We need an antidote!
Without sarsaparilla? Without FAKE sarsaparilla, I can't do anything!
And in the meantime, the real Clockwork Smurf is in danger!
That's right! Let's go rescue him first!
TO ARMS, SMURFIZENS!
But, we don't have any weapons!
Bring whatever!
My pitchfork, for smurf's sake!
My rolling pin!
My mirror!
My butterfly net!
Has anybody seen my bottlesmurf!
Are you ready?
MOVE OUT!
At the same time...
That imbecile Gargamel will be happy!
The Smurf! Where's the Smurf?
The fake Clockwork Smurf! Handy Smurf arrived too late!
12

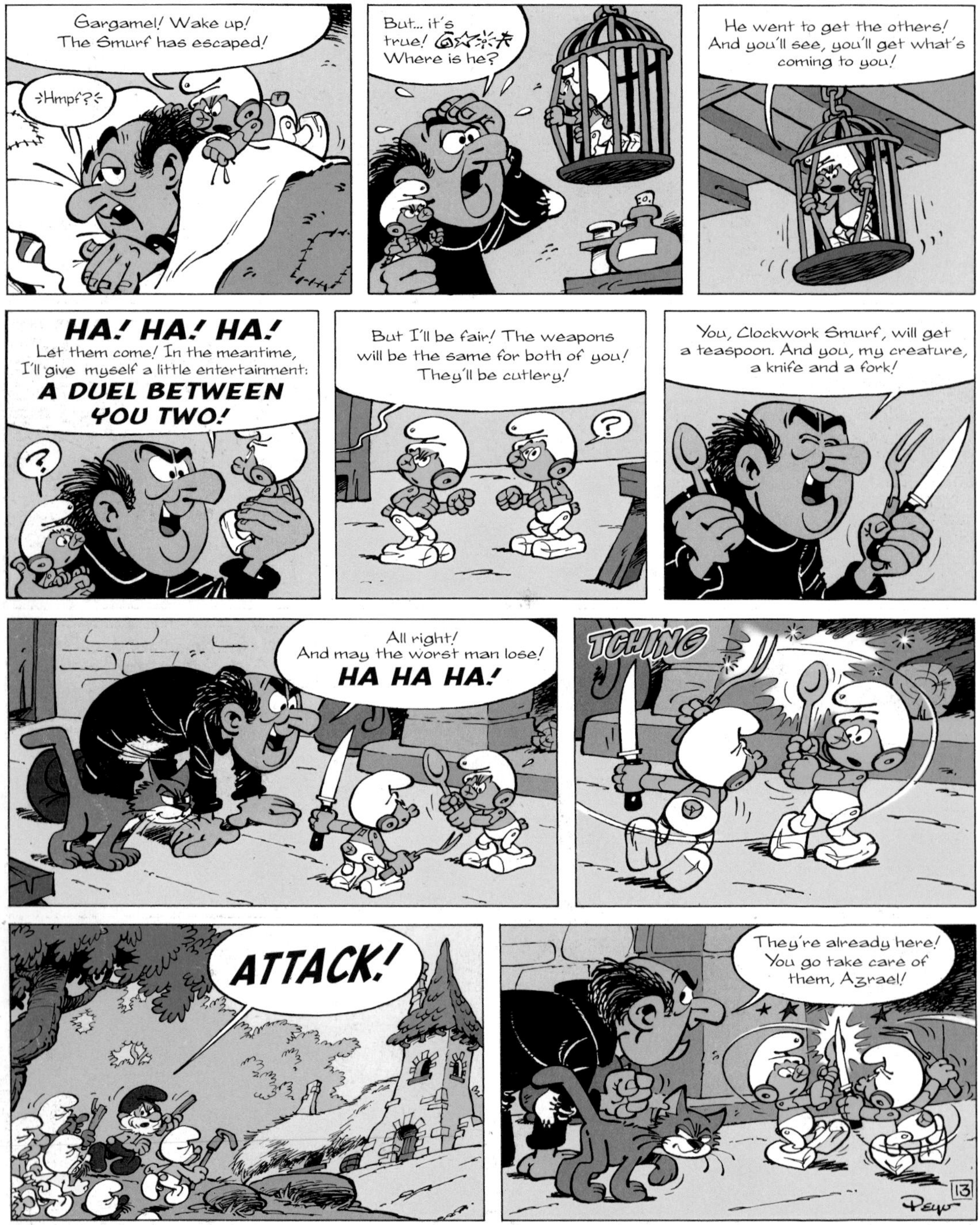
Gargamel! Wake up! The Smurf has escaped!
Hmpf?
But... it's true! Where is he?
He went to get the others! And you'll see, you'll get what's coming to you!
HA! HA! HA! Let them come! In the meantime, I'll give myself a little entertainment: A DUEL BETWEEN YOU TWO!
?
But I'll be fair! The weapons will be the same for both of you! They'll be cutlery!
?
You, Clockwork Smurf, will get a teaspoon. And you, my creature, a knife and a fork!
All right! And may the worst man lose! HA HA HA!
TCHING
ATTACK!
They're already here! You go take care of them, Azrael!
13
Peyo

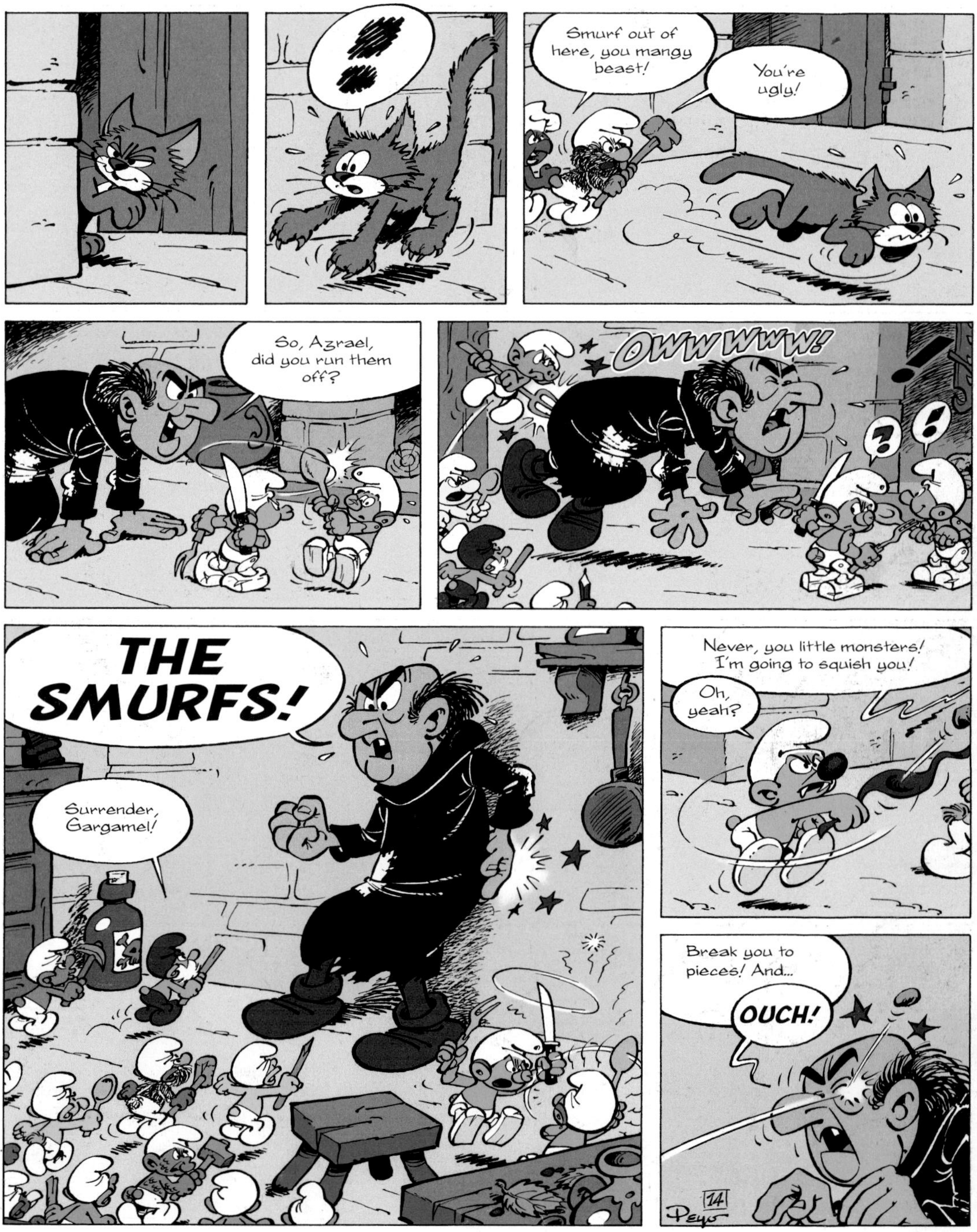

Smurf out of here, you mangy beast!
You're ugly!
So, Azrael, did you run them off?
OWWWWW!
?
!
THE SMURFS!
Surrender, Gargamel!
Never, you little monsters! I'm going to squish you!
Oh, yeah?
Break you to pieces! And...
OUCH!
14
Peyo

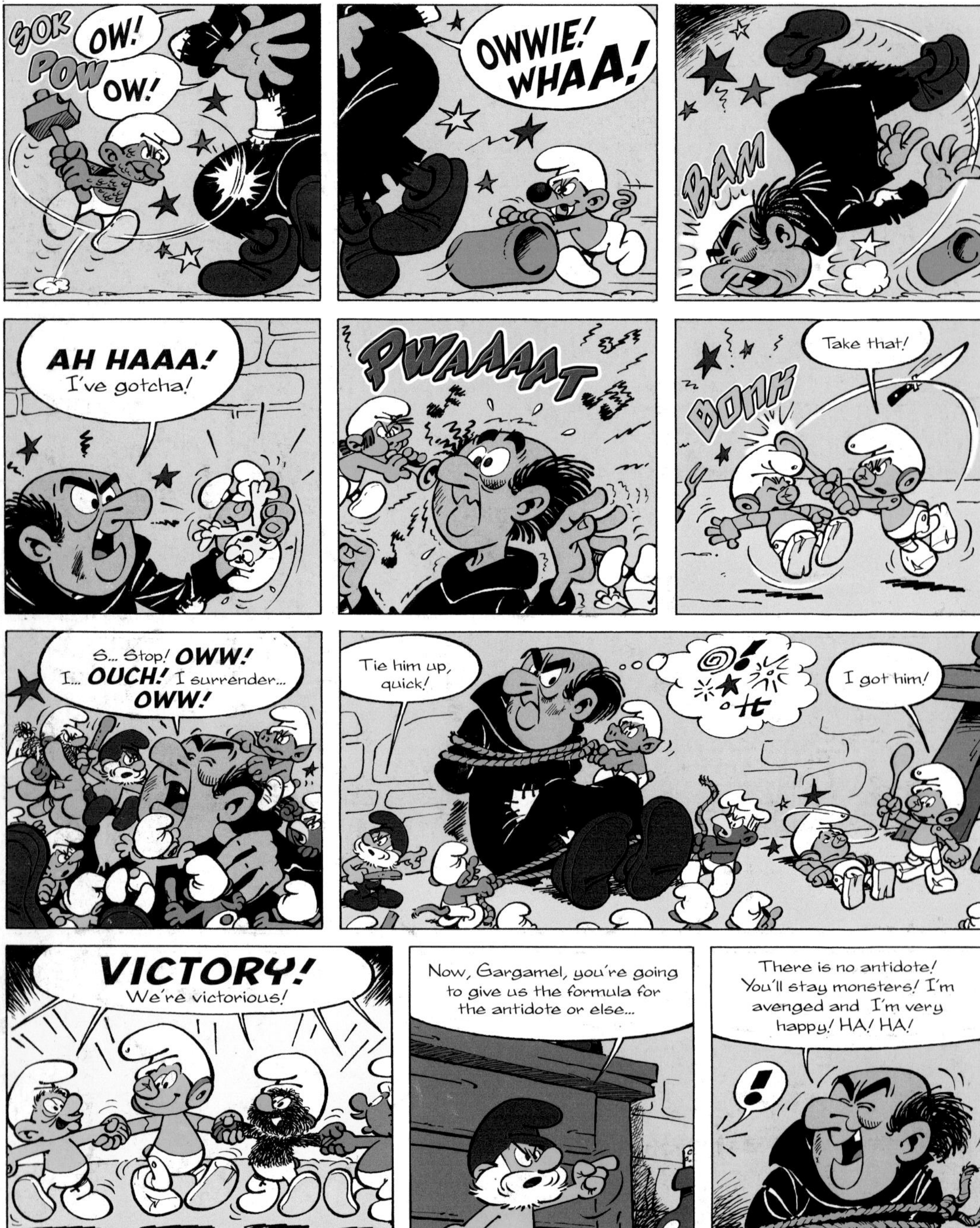
SOK
OW!
POW
OW!
OWWIE! WHAA!
BAM
AH HAAA! I've gotcha!
PWAAAAT
Take that!
BONK
S... Stop! OWW! I... OUCH! I surrender... OWW!
Tie him up, quick!
I got him!
VICTORY! We're victorious!
Now, Gargamel, you're going to give us the formula for the antidote or else...
There is no antidote! You'll stay monsters! I'm avenged and I'm very happy! HA! HA!
!
15

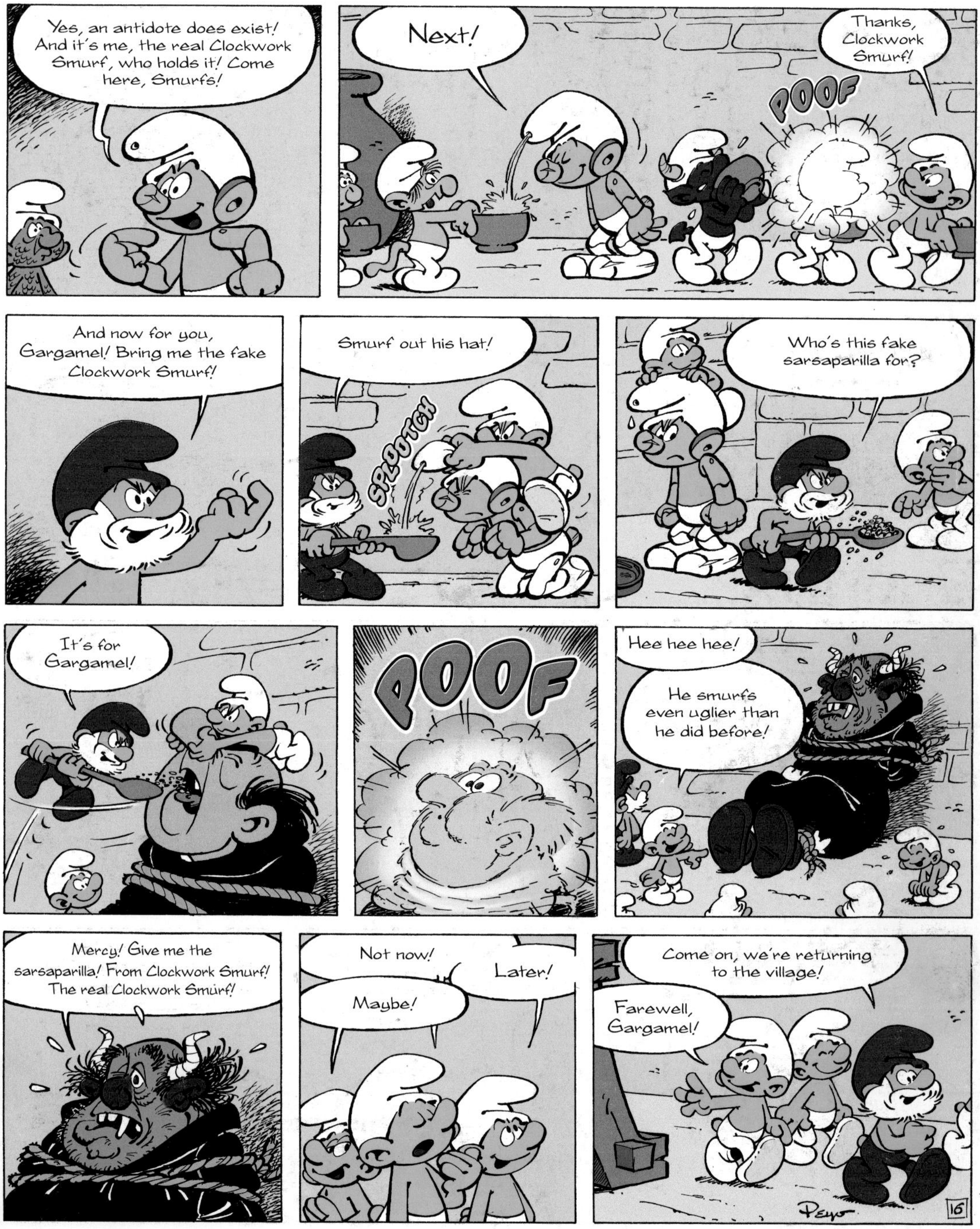

Yes, an antidote does exist! And it's me, the real Clockwork Smurf, who holds it! Come here, Smurfs!
Next!
POOF
Thanks, Clockwork Smurf!
And now for you, Gargamel! Bring me the fake Clockwork Smurf!
Smurf out his hat!
SPLOOTCH
Who's this fake sarsaparilla for?
It's for Gargamel!
POOF
Hee hee hee!
He smurfs even uglier than he did before!
Mercy! Give me the sarsaparilla! From Clockwork Smurf! The real Clockwork Smurf!
Not now!
Later!
Maybe!
Come on, we're returning to the village!
Farewell, Gargamel!
Peyo
16

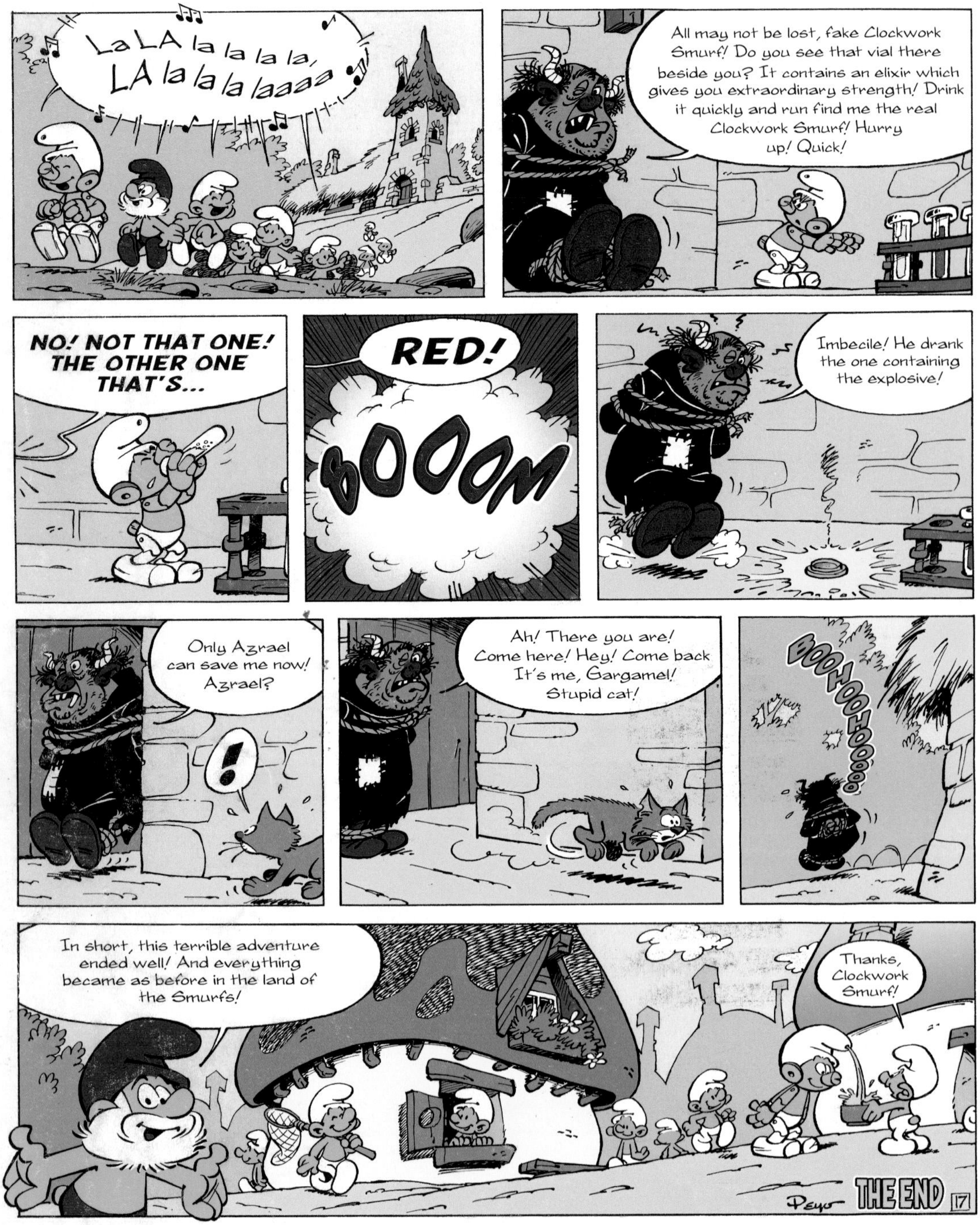
La LA la la la la,
LA la la la laaaa
All may not be lost, fake Clockwork Smurf! Do you see that vial there beside you? It contains an elixir which gives you extraordinary strength! Drink it quickly and run find me the real Clockwork Smurf! Hurry up! Quick!
NO! NOT THAT ONE! THE OTHER ONE THAT'S...
RED!
BOOOM
Imbecile! He drank the one containing the explosive!
Only Azrael can save me now! Azrael?
!
Ah! There you are! Come here! Hey! Come back It's me, Gargamel! Stupid cat!
BOOHOOHOOOOO
In short, this terrible adventure ended well! And everything became as before in the land of the Smurfs!
Thanks, Clockwork Smurf!
Peyo
THE END
17